The Mimic's Own Voice

a novella by

Tom Williams

MAIN STREET RAG PUBLISHING COMPANY
CHARLOTTE, NORTH CAROLINA

Library of Congress Control Number: 2011923701

ISBN: 978-1-59948-294-1

Produced in the United States of America

Main Street Rag
PO Box 690100
Charlotte, NC 28227
www.MainStreetRag.com

To my mother, Susan Williams
1944-2010

The Mimic's Own Voice

In the halcyon days of professional mimics, shortly after they'd outpaced their predecessors, the vernacular storytellers, who had, a decade earlier, wrested the comedic throne from the one-liner royalty, it would have been difficult to name a town of ten thousand souls that didn't possess some venue where performed those artists who made their fame and fortune with stunning mimicry of the period's political leaders and actors, athletes and musicians, scholars, and men of science. And at every performance inside those theaters, whether located in the Badger or Beaver State, all seats were filled, as were the aisles and exits, prompting accounts of fire marshals arriving with the intent of stopping the show, only to get so caught up in their own laughter and enjoyment that they would forget their professional function as disperser of those bunched so close together as to create a hazard. Even the streets and sidewalks outside the theaters: they would be massed by citizens who'd shown up too late to purchase tickets yet wouldn't depart; those closest pressed their ears to the doors and relayed to the others the identity of whomever the mimic was, in the parlance of the trade, "doing." And though many couldn't hear a word from inside the theater, they could content themselves with memories of routines,

reveling in their proximity to the men whose altered voices
entertained them during radio and television broadcasts
every night.

To many of today's lay comedy fans, the names of these
mimics are mostly forgotten, yet in no way should that
diminish their celebrity. Banks, the enormous man whose
voice could flutter as high as a soprano's, then, in seconds,
plunge to the rumble of a bass. O'Meara, who began life
in an orphanage, where he pioneered his "Dialogue Act,"
the pairing of two disparate celebrities—a governor and a
gigolo—in an absurd conversation. Never once did he flub
or misspeak. He always maintained a pure pair of voices,
as if he could speak from both sides of his mouth. And
Salvatore, who, at the height of his popularity, would be
shot by a jealous lover, but until then, sang in the voices of
the era's best romantic crooners—better than the crooners,
some said—and boasted of seducing thousands of women
and not an inconsiderable number of men. (All this despite
his five-foot height and a set of teeth no dentist had ever
seen.) And, of course, Hernandez, the genius, who with his
"Impromptu" shifted from celebrities to audience members
as his subjects (though his mimicry of celebrities was as
perfect as a recording); even when it was discovered that
the real people whose voices he reproduced were indeed
part of a paid entourage, no one could say his talents were
fewer than he'd portrayed, only that his spontaneity was
less than presented. After the brief scandal that attended
this discovery—worse for mimics, in some respects, than
Salvatore's shooting—Hernandez returned to celebrities, on
occasion trumping O'Meara's "Dialogue," with four- or five-
way conversations, never once losing track of whose voice
he was to match his to, and his fortunes barely crested.

These giants cast tremendous shadows, in which
numerous others toiled and thrived, most of their names
lost even to the most meticulous of Comedic Studies
scholars today, yet it is plain that this period represented the

mimics' greatest triumph, a time when the most hubristic never considered that they'd wear out their welcome and be replaced, just as they'd dispatched the vernacular storytellers. But, by and by, the audiences for the mimics diminished and turned increasingly toward the next group of up and comers, a group of young men whose penetrating satires and caustic wits earned them the label of the social critics.

But perhaps the greatest of all mimics did not perform during these grand old days. By the time of his birth, the social critics had set the table for their own downfall, and those earning the bulk of the nation's applause were the observational comics, they who charmed with brash, often profane humor, taut timing, and the pungent accuracy of their commentary. Overheard, now and again, from critics who'd straddled the three distinct decades, was the argument that mimics fell from grace because even with their different acts they all did the same thing: duplicate voices. The social critics had variety to their material, but they too became indistinguishable from one another, as they shared the same targets, and one can only complain about the government or intolerance or consumerism in a limited number of ways. It was, finally, the observational comics who aimed their jabs in a direction that promised endless notoriety: at the people themselves. "No matter where you go," wrote one anonymous editorial writer, "laughter spills out of private homes, enormous theaters and tiny taverns, as long as the featured performer keeps his material fresh. And as long as the subject is ordinary human foibles, it seems the observational comic has an endless supply."

At this time, not only did the mimics no longer command the stage, most had succumbed to old age and disease, leaving behind only O'Meara, and uncovered in a series of articles appearing in the *National Herald Daily* was this unsettling fact: the eighty-seven year old dressed each morning in his cutaway tux, pinned a dead orchid to his lapel, and waited by the phone for a call from his agent, a man who'd died in a boating accident twenty years previous. The next week, this tragedy found its way into some observational comics' routines, who capped jokes with lines such as this: "If the phone rings, will he even know which voice to answer in?" (Quietly, a month after the articles, O'Meara passed away, and his funeral, paid for by an anonymous patron, was attended by two people: a Presbyterian minister and the nursing home orderly who'd found O'Meara dead.) Such jokes typified the new breed of comic: in virtually everything they found a punch line, including the last days of addled mimics. After O'Meara's death, critics and comics both predicted mimicry would go by way of knock-knock jokes, which scholars today consider the advent of professional comedy but haven't been heard on stage since the days of long beards and virgin brides. And at that point, who could disagree? Bernard Sikes, a prototypical observational comic who performed in the days of the social critics, would claim, "Life is funnier than any joke you could make up," a fact borne out by a glance at the newspapers of the day. Shortly after the O'Meara incident, one read of top-level government figures taking bribes and evangelists caught with mistresses—the standard fare of social critics—but also of neighbors in subdivisions shooting at one another during property line feuds, housewives operating gambling parlors in basements, teens hijacking city buses and toddlers trading baby sisters for puppies. At such a time, who could foresee anything like a return to those days of tuxedo-clad men behind bulky microphones, turning their backs to the audience, then turning around to reveal disguised voices that embraced the stammers, lisps and strangled vowels of their subjects?

Still and all, it was into this environment that Douglas Myles was born. Years later, when it was whispered he possessed powers defying explanation, some facetiously speculated he must have willed his birth in these times in order to provide himself the challenge he craved. And though few considered this charge seriously, none could deny there were aspects of the man that made such a legend appropriate, legend being the preferred method of dealing with the spectacular figure, as it confirms he has a fantastic means of acquiring his talents, to which the average mortal has no access.

When he first emerged in the spotlight, and throughout his professional career—a total of just over seven years— little was known about his background, which allowed speculation and intrigue to surround him like air; but thankfully a manuscript was discovered in his former house two years ago, ten years after his death, by a team of students led by the comedy historian Anton Greene. In the years that the two-bedroom townhouse had been restored and opened to the public, the manuscript and other papers had been hiding in plain sight. "One of the kids," Greene claims, "found a battered-looking umbrella file in storage!" Myles's composition of it has been authenticated by a number of peer-reviewed studies, thus replacing the dubious and unauthorized biographies that sprang up after his death, as Greene joked, "like mushrooms following a spring rain." In their assemblages of rumor and ill-fashioned fiction, those biographers would have one believe Myles was a runaway reared by a family of mesmerists, or that he grew up with an aboriginal grandfather in an adobe, surrounded by little other than the sound of his own voice and the wisdom of the ancients. But they are out of print now and should probably be mentioned as little as possible.

Myles's manuscript, housed now at The Pratt-Falls Center, Dr. Greene's home institution, excited laymen and scholars at first, for all suspected it had been written for publication. Yet no contract exists among Myles's papers (and, as the reader shall see, he was quite the saver), nor can one be found in the files of any publishers. This increased speculation that a bidding war for its rights would take place, though after the manuscript's seventy-three handwritten pages were initially read, no offers, save for the Pratt-Falls's, were forthcoming. From its curious usage of second person, to its enigmatic opening and closing lines, "Your name is Douglas Myles . . . . They never really listened," it does not divulge entirely his secrets, while it raises mysteries all its own. Still, there are a host of details which offer, for the first time, a definitive glimpse into his early life.

He was born in the Middle West, in a middle-sized city, known primarily then and now as a test market for fast food restaurants, the only child of Angela and Ellis Myles, a black mother and white father. In those days, such a combination was virtually unheard of, as, at the time of their only son's birth, the Myles's union was only three years away from being illegal in many states. Now one sees such couples and their beautiful broods of children and hardly notices; some insist that interracial marriages will further increase due to Myles's manuscript, as hopeful parents attempt to capture a genius as immense and profitable as his in their scions. However, Myles, during his life, never spoke of this openly. His parents died when he was eighteen, killed in a car crash, the fault of an intoxicated driver named Grimes. But to those few who knew him, such as Lamar Jackson, the famed black comic, and those who simply knew of him, he said he was a light-skinned black man. According to Peter Szok, who along with Anton Greene is considered the dean of contemporary Comedic Studies, this demi-fabrication signals in part why his mimicry may have been so singular and accurate, as Myles never stopped practicing. "Even in day to day affairs," Szok states, "he was mimicking someone he was not." Those who sought to ascribe a political motivation to Myles's self-identification as black were overjoyed to discover his parents' community activism—in particular his social-worker mother—but were disappointed by the following: "It was easier to tell people you were black." Easier than what, many wonder. But, as the reader shall see, simple answers are rarely forthcoming when the subject is Douglas Myles.

Myles also writes that he knew of his gift for mimicry as soon as he could speak, but he did not share it at first. "You could hear everyone speaking. Your mother, father, your Gran and great-aunts, your uncle from Arkansas. He told stories about giant alligators and raffish river otters. And you could isolate each voice, separating them from the others like tracks on a tape. Whenever you wanted to hear them again, even if they were back in Arkansas with the gators and otters, you could concentrate and hear exactly what they said." For some time he didn't think this was at all strange, primarily because the only people he knew in his early youth were his maternal relatives. Rarely did he and his parents spend time away from their small home. He makes no mention of his parents' friends. Not once was the little family graced by a visit from his father's wealthy family. But when he moved on to kindergarten, young Douglas would discover that as well as being the only child of an interracial marriage—the class, though, was somewhat integrated—he was also the only one with his gift. This he relays in a charming scene, early on in the manuscript: "A dark-skinned boy approached you at the table. He was interested to know where you lived and what your father did for a living. His family owned a house two streets south of yours; his father worked at the oleo plant. After a few more minutes, you asked him how often he listened to the voices in his head. He didn't get to answer, because your teacher laid her hand on your shoulder and asked what the voices told you to do.

"'Nothing,' you said. 'They just talk.'"

"'They don't tell you to set fires or harm small animals?'

"You shook your head, smiling, noticing without effort that her voice, normally as sturdy as the brick schoolhouse, quavered, then rose and fell. After she asked, 'You're sure about that?', your lips parted to shape your voice to hers, but something told you this wasn't the time or place, that you shouldn't tell anyone else about the voices and what you could do with them."

If for no reason than the above passage, Comedic Studies scholars would be ecstatic about the manuscript's existence, yet there is more, each successive page filled with evidence of two things primarily. One, that, aside from the cross-cultural upbringing and occasional sense of alienation— due to a skin color and talent no one else shared—Myles had a fairly normal childhood. None of his schools catered to the excessively privileged or prodigiously talented; he was the product of a public school as overcrowded and underfunded as any from that period of time. He earned good but not spectacular grades in subjects he enjoyed— history, speech, Spanish, and literature—though his father, Ellis, a community college algebra instructor, "insisted that if you only applied yourself you'd do better in math and science." "Imagine," crows Anton Greene, "Douglas Myles, hailed so often that one rarely said his name without some honorific preceding or following it, lectured in the same manner as so many underachievers!" But, in addition, his ordinary life is revealed in the pages that display him as an avid TV watcher, able at the time of his composition to remember from his youth the sequence of network shows Monday through Friday, as well as a host of Saturday morning cartoons. While no athlete, he was not picked on overmuch, and he did ride a bike, a mode of transport he used to get from his house to the comedy clubs later on. In brief, he was as ordinary a toddler as he was a youth, as undistinguished an adolescent as he was a teen.

This leads, though, to the second area of evidence, or actual lack of it, which is likely a reason why the publishers who had prepared huge bids for the manuscript lost interest after reading it: nowhere does Myles present a step-by-step manual for how to become a mimic, nor does he detail a chance meeting with a mysterious Tibetan monk, skilled at the art of vocal chord manipulation. No magic. No training regimen, no complex system of verbal calisthenics to maintain his skills. Banks, it's been said, gargled with warm salt water every morning to keep his voice supple, whereas O'Meara drank no beverage warmer than tepid, and before each performance Salvatore said the alphabet in Portuguese, Italian and English, forward and backward. From Myles one finds nothing like these rituals, though he does briefly comment on them, knowing, as he did, as much about his forebears as today's scholars. He opines: "They were nervous. They feared the day their talent would be gone or that they'd find one voice they couldn't do. (They didn't know the greatest risk.) So to make themselves feel safe, they invented elaborate gimmicks and superstitions. You never needed any." The ominous nature of that parenthesis aside, one surely sees in this quote a man whose confidence in his ability never wavered. One thing Myles insists upon throughout the manuscript—in the few taped interviews one hears similar statements—is that his talent was equal parts a gift from a kindly deity and an accident of genetics. But he guessed that the best thing a budding mimic could have was a house full of people, their voices lifted in squabble or delight.

For most readers, the manuscript's greatest value is when Myles turns from his early years to the beginnings of his performances. Though on his ascendance to the first stage of his popularity it may have appeared he'd been an overnight success, he had to find his way through a succession of small venues, confront a hostile audience or two and on occasion tell himself that he wasn't good enough. His first audience was, naturally, his family, and they encouraged him to perform at every function where more than a few members gathered. "They told you of Banks, Salvatore, O'Meara and Hernandez, but also Simpkins, the one black mimic, and compared you to him because you both could do the voices of white and black folk." (Had Myles not have known of him, it's very likely Simpkins would be one of the forgotten, instead of, as he is now, considered one of the true masters, as well as a primary influence on Myles.) Moreover, his family members were most pleased when he would imitate those relatives who were not present at the time. "Do Freddy, they'd shout. Your Cousin Bailey. Your Aunt Jane. And each voice that came from your mouth fetched more laughter than the last." One by one, though, his family members departed this earth, leaving him each year with a smaller audience, and fewer voices to duplicate. Soon, it seemed, the only place where his family spoke was in his head, but no one, including him, wanted to laugh anymore. Thus, when his parents died, it was not to professional comedy that he turned. He writes, "You needed to make money. You needed to find a job that paid."

And so he did, as a shelver at the public library, a modern edifice of six stories and parking decks that now bears a wing named in his memory and is among the most visited structures in the Buckeye State. (An early report that his ghost wanders the stacks has been recently exposed as a PR agent's fabrication.) At the time of his hiring, no one would have surmised that he'd do more for the library than he was supposed to: stack and reshelve books from eight to four-thirty, with a half hour for lunch at noon. "He was the most nondescript fellow," said one of his coworkers after his celebrated first appearance on the *H.H. McCormick Show*. "Sometimes he didn't say a word for a whole day." The minimum wage earnings, so paltry at the time, just kept him in groceries and patched his trousers and inner tubes. The only material thing left him by his parents was the ranch house they lived in, and it had several payments remaining. (Sadly, this building, which Myles describes as having "rooms which could barely fit us all," was razed two months after he left. His colossal fame did not materialize in time to slow his hometown's urban renewal plans.) He wrote to his father's family, who expressed sympathy, but did little for him, as they'd experienced financial turnarounds and, as they never recognized his father's marriage or Douglas's birth, they had themselves to take care of—the few aunts and uncles and their children, all of whom Myles would never meet, even when he may have been the most famous man alive. Living prudently, he managed, and, after a year and an extension from a kindly loan officer—rarer than a dodo in that age—he paid off the house, though he continued to live in the same fashion, as he'd gotten only one raise from the library, and an additional fifty cents an hour bought little more than extra bags of rice or beans to place in his meager cupboard.

Biking to work in all weather, shelving mysteries and cookbooks, biographies and science fiction classics, occasionally training at the checkout desk, then biking home, where he ate simple dinners and snacked on dried fruit, Myles lived out his years between eighteen and twenty. He rarely went out, for which in later years he was grateful, as his Spartan existence prevented him from cultivating a taste for drink, drug or smoke—traps for comics as long as one could get paid for a punch line. Out of economy, he developed no romantic interests (despite the claims of offspring filed by desperate women in supermarket newspapers); he had friendly neighbors and colleagues at work, some of whom would at the height of his fame maintain they'd been great friends, but none could describe the interior of his house or name the brand of bike he rode. What he did away from work was practice. "An empty house," he writes, "that was once so loud with voices, can make anybody blue. The TV can fill it up, but you can't make it speak the way you want. So, after two years, you started to open your mouth again and let the voices emerge." Not only was it strange, he affirmed, to perform in an empty home, it was odd to be talking, as he spoke so little at work. And here is likely an image that will dampen the eyes of the most objective of scholars: twenty-year-old Myles, thin as the pasta he boiled in his one pot, with a shaved head—the only haircut he knew how to administer—standing in the middle of a tidy but empty living room, brightening the darkness and chasing away the silence by reproducing the voices of his dead relations. "It was easy to do, after a few moments of recalling. All of them had some aspect to their voice that made it like snowflakes or fingerprints, unlike any other. Father's harsh tenor. Mom's smoky trill. Uncle Derek's broken whisper. The warm brass of Gran."

Szok and Greene both hold that Myles's being able to live in this house was fortuitous, as had he been forced into an apartment, especially of the kind he could afford, he might have been quieted by neighbors working odd hours and trying to sleep or turned in by busybodies as a lunatic who spoke to himself in as many different voices as there were days in the month. But this practice had, at first, no end in Myles's mind. He was not preparing, he was not refining, he was not dreaming of a career that would whisk him around the nation, deposit him on stages where once divas sang and actors declaimed. He was simply trying, in his words, "to keep close to those who'd left you behind and fill the emptiness with joy."

Working still at the library, he thought about college, at times picking up brochures listing night classes at junior colleges or adult education centers. But he never believed he'd have the time or finances to devote himself to study in the manner he felt best. Later on, this surprised most, as he appeared erudite in interviews and on stage, so much so that a certain reporter at an august magazine attempted to track down the name Douglas Myles or a revealing alias among the registrar's rolls of colleges and universities. (Nothing ever came of this search, save for embarrassment on the once-cocksure reporter's part.) Myles would, however, discover a hoard of film reels in the library's media center —at least sixty hours' worth—that featured those famed mimics whom he drew comparisons to while performing before his family. Of course, he'd never seen them before; only O'Meara was alive when Myles was growing up, and the only time his name was mentioned before his death was in the jokes of the observational comics. None can be certain that had Myles not stumbled across these films he wouldn't have gone on to his first attempts as a performer; he himself comments that the films were "fortunate, but you thought, without pride, you could do better." However, upon his discovery, he began staying after work to watch these films, as well as checking them out along with a projector, using at home a blank wall for a screen. "For hours you watched them, admiring the tuxes, marveling at their command, wondering if perhaps you'd been born at the wrong time."

Relying on the events leading up to this discovery, no one would comment that Myles had experienced a charmed life, what with all he and his family endured; yet the serendipity of the library he worked at having all these films seems, at least, a sign of fortunes beginning to change, as if, at last, a friendly hand descended from the heavens to set things aright. Needless to say, any student of Myles will tell you, shortly after the films appeared in his life, he started to show an ambitious turn, and desired to try—"at least one attempt"—to better those long-dead lions of mimicry, no longer in the privacy of home, but on some stage. As his fear of being born at the wrong time evinces, he knew it would not be a simple task, finding the right venue for his debut. But he was wise beyond his age—he was still only twenty—and quickly concluded that the comedy club was not for him, even though, as Greene's research shows, there were seventeen such places in his hometown then. Instead, his debut occurred at a former warehouse called, enigmatically, The Hub (now too, sadly, destroyed). Myles didn't know why it bore that name, as he'd never been; it was located across town from his home, in the one section that might be called bohemian or progressive. The patrons dressed in black, he recalls, and the cool cement walls of the space were covered with original paintings, most of which flew right by him in terms of meaning or intent. One sculpture, he remembered, stood near the men's room and consisted of hubcaps (the source of the club's name, one wonders), a shopping cart, aluminum softball bats, and a Moose Lodge fez. #14, it was titled. Clearly, the Hub was as avant-garde as a middle-sized city in the Buckeye State could get, even though, relying on Myles's depiction, Peter Szok attests that most of these artists and their work would have underwhelmed the urbane crowds of Manhattan or Pittsburgh. The night of Myles's debut was an open-mic affair that he'd read about in the entertainment supplement of the *Dispatch*, and he determined this was a venue in which, even if he failed miserably—and for this fate he was prepared—he doubted he'd see in the audience a neighbor or co-worker; hence, no one would know of it, save for the grim crowd who appeared "likely to forget you as soon as you walked on stage."

Of course, such was not the case. With his allotted fifteen minutes, Myles performed between a pale young man in a diaper who railed oedipally for seven minutes, then babbled in a "guttural baby talk of plosives and fricatives until he collapsed," and an equally pale young man who wheezed in and out of a harmonica while strumming a guitar and bellowing a song that rhymed "capitalist" with "I am pissed" and "free market" and "aw fuck it." When Myles stepped out on stage, blinking at the bright light, he was wearing hand me downs from various male relatives: a double-windsor knotted tie with too much blue for his brown jacket and white shirt, brown corduroys and hard soled shoes—"the closest thing you had to a tux." All the patrons were white, but he expected that, knowing few persons of color ventured into this part of town. In fact, in his racially mixed neighborhood, especially when he was of school age, the district housing The Hub was pejoratively called, "Boy's Town," and warned against as a place where young men like himself were seduced by wicked and slavering homosexuals. On this night, though, Myles was unconcerned with such rumors. And it is probably best to allow his own account to speak here, as it is one of the few instances where he evokes a scene of personal triumph. As well, it shows how, years later, this performance probably cheered Myles more than any other, save for his early forays with family voices.

He writes, "You couldn't see anyone, but you weren't looking, either. Had you seen any one face distinctly, you might have lost your voice, as the nerves hadn't settled. You halfway convinced yourself your family had been too kind and your own ear was deaf to real speech. But you said, in your own voice, 'My name is Douglas Myles, and I'm a mimic.' You paused, hoping to hear some applause or interest. Instead, you heard bodies shifting, chairs creaking. A cool breeze stirred. From the back, a voice called, 'What is this? "The Sam Mack Variety Hour?"' You knew this was meant to heckle. But in that voice, with its wheezing smoker's catches, you could tell the speaker was older. He knew of that TV show where all the greats had gotten their start. No one else laughed, because no one knew what the heckler was talking about. But he'd unintentionally played right into your hand, providing you a perfect introduction to your 'act'—if it could be called that then.

"'But it is, sir,' you said, in Sam Mack's briny heehaw of a cackle, 'and may I have the pleasure of introducing a mimic you'll be getting to know a lot of, believe me. And his name is Patrick O'Meara.'

"The room remained silent. Another chill wind breezed past, ruffling your tie a little. You pressed it against your shirt and stared at the shadows before you. You didn't turn your back, as all of them had, from O'Meara to Hernandez, except in the 'Dialogue Act.' About that you were certain. You wouldn't bug your eyes or muss your hair or slip on glasses or a pair of false teeth. It would be the voice alone.

It was time to 'do' O'Meara, but not any of his impressions. Rather, you'd whisper in that plaintive, tipsy manner he used between them. When you were finished, someone gasped. The heckler. And you and he, for a moment, both knew you sounded exactly like O'Meara leading up to his opening impression of the then-president on the golf tee. But soon you went back to Sam Mack introducing Salvatore. You could do his dropped consonants and liquid vowels in your sleep. Silence filled the room, as it did when you tried Banks's alarm clock laughter and Simpkins's tinny stammer. Your fifteen minutes were up. Then in Sam Mack's voice you uttered his signature closing: 'It's been a peach, folks. Now can it!' You followed that with your own voice, saying goodnight. Applause came, politely from most, but in a racket from the back. He knew. You knew. It was time to begin."

Myles appeared at The Hub for two months. He was featured a few times, especially after some enterprising member of the staff showed old footage of the same mimics as evidence that this curious young fellow had captured not only what the men said—Banks's poor-mouthing, Hernandez's carefully mangled Spanglish—but exactly how they spoke. On one of these nights, Myles was caught backstage by the manager of another "alternative space," Either/Or, where guitar and accordion punk combos performed side by side with latex lingerie shows, and it would be on this stage where Myles began to attract a following that numbered in the hundreds. "Perhaps all the avant-garde in the state," he jokes. Peter Szok asserts that, along with his undeniable talents, his timing was impeccable, as in such spaces as the Hub and Either/Or, the denizens were growing increasingly fond of the fashions of the decade in which mimics flourished. The vintage, narrow-lapel, one button jackets, tropical island shirts and angora sweaters had begun to take up rack room in the used clothing stores nearby (though elsewhere the fad was fading), and to find what seemed in Myles an authentic purveyor of the humor of that period, for these local hipsters, was a boon they'd never imagined. "As a purveyor of retro-kitsch," Szok concludes, "was how he was first appreciated."

Among others, Szok, ever the aesthete, believes this phase of Myles's to be his finest as an artist. His concept was so pure, so esoteric and singular, he represented an entire movement, as none came before or after him—who'd thought to mimic the mimics? During his later career, those who had seen him in these early performances—fifteen to thirty minutes long, at best—would complain that his work, like so many others, had been corrupted and commodified as he moved on to larger venues and appeared on popular TV programs, but this is the subject of some debate, as are Szok and his camp's assertions. About this earlier period, Myles affirms: "You knew you could do better."

At this point—surrounded by devotees whose admiration was great while their numbers were small—one sees an event like the appearance of a mysterious stranger into Myles's life. (Though one wonders why there's such a need for such an encounter; it seems, if anything, that an incident of this type ruins the totality of his story, which, like many of this nation, privileges such virtues as hard work, persistence and integrity, and allows for the toothsome spice of good fortune.) For during one of the performances at Either/Or, Myles was approached by an assistant for Clayton Adams III, the chief comedy critic of the *Dispatch*. As in the case of the films, one wonders if this moment brought him to his fame or if it merely expedited his development. It also signals, especially in Myles's own mind, more of the special light that emerged in his life; for the assistant, a young woman named Therese Morton, caught him just as he was headed toward the exit, pushing his bike along the tile floor. Ms. Morton, who, at 82, conducted an interview with Anton Greene, insisted that Myles did not slow down as she called his name and ran toward him. She said, "He looked afraid, as if no one had ever spoken his name in anything but anger." Briefly, Myles treats the occasion, pointing out that despite the clamorous and growing crowds that witnessed his mimicry and skirmished to meet with him backstage, he never stayed long after a routine. About this, he would maintain the same attitude his entire career, departing the stage, then hightailing it back to whatever hotel he stayed in. "What they want to tell you," he writes in a later section, "is that you're wonderful and talented and unlike any other. And you didn't want to listen to that. You didn't want to believe them, because that seemed dangerous."

Still, on this particular night, Ms. Morton caught up with him, despite the fact she was not supposed to be at Either/Or. She was supposed to be downtown at the Laughter Lounge, viewing a pair of nationally renowned comedians, Mr. Motormouth and the aforementioned Bernard Sikes (on his last tour before his death), in order to supply her boss with the grist necessary for his review. (Among Middle Western comedy critics, Clayton Adams III was particularly tough; he was known as the "Man Who Never Laughed.") Yet she'd heard so much about the odd young man whose act defied categorization, and she figured she could catch his performance and make it back in time to see Mr. Motormouth. ("Sikes's act hadn't changed in years," she claimed.) Describing Myles, she said, "Though many, myself included, had nothing to go on as to how accurate a mimic he was, the many different voices he produced assured us completely." Offstage, the man was anything but assured. By the time Ms. Morton caught up with him, he'd pushed open the exit door with his front tire and was about to seat himself on his bike. "Wait," she called. "I must speak with you." This request was met with a blank expression and Myles opening wider the exit door. Ms. Morton, later on, would say, "I couldn't let him go, though I suppose I could have come back another night. Yet, after such an incredible performance, how could I wait? I yelled, 'You need to play at a bigger house!'

"'Pardon?' he said, very politely, in a voice so unassuming, I could scarcely believe that voice could produce anything but itself.

"'You absolutely need to perform at some of the clubs,' I said. He paused and blinked. He didn't know who I was, if I were deranged or an ordinary fan. Then he got on his bike, looked over his shoulder, and said, 'You're too kind.'"

As stated before, Myles rarely tries, in the manuscript, to set scenes or recreate formative moments. Here lies another likely reason why the document that once prompted publishers to raid their cash reserves for an advance, still sits under review at the Pratt-Falls Center. But what he does write is telling: "You would later find that the woman worked for the *Dispatch*. But at the time, knowing this wouldn't have mattered. Her voice—a cool ivory—pushed you, but you were already on your way."

They never met again. Although it would be six months more before he would leave the clubs of his hometown, and Therese Morton tried to see him after other shows, he proved to be as elusive as a fugitive. Also, Clayton Adams III had many more tasks for his assistant, so many that she'd eventually resign and not return to the newspaper world. It's worth saying, though, that when Anton Greene showed her a copy of the manuscript, Ms. Morton admitted her day was made when she saw Myles's description of her voice. "I only wished I'd heard it from his mouth," she said.

Even with Therese Morton's ringing endorsement, an increased confidence and a talent that was growing each day, finding new voices to reproduce though he stuck with the mimics in his act, Myles did not immediately ingratiate himself in the hearts of his hometown's traditional comedy audiences. He leapt past the smoky taverns with exposed brick walls, odiferous urinals and poor PA systems, and he auditioned for a club called the Giggle Room, owned by one Lewis Denboski, who, at 77, was old enough not to simply remember Banks, O'Meara, et al, but to have operated the Giggle Room under a previous name of the Copycat Club. Beneath the many black and white photos of social critics and observational comics that festooned his walls, one might find a glossy of Salvatore or Simpkins, and the one of Hernandez Myles especially liked, with the tuxedo-clad master standing next to a plain-looking woman in a boxy dress, about to "spontaneously" duplicate her voice. It took him a total of five minutes to audition before Denboski, in which he did Sam Mack (whose voice he was growing tired of: "it seemed like too much of a conceit"), Banks and O'Meara. Prepared to do Simpkins, in particular his stammering introductions that amplified how sure his voice was during an impression, Myles was surprised to see Denboski standing and clapping. "I should keep you around just to remind me of the old days," he said.

Generous of spirit, praise, and cash, Denboski became what one might call Myles's first and only manager. Their relationship, though brief, begins with Myles's two-week stint at the Giggle Room, where, he summarizes, "Only Mr. Denboski laughed. The audience stared and said, 'What's so funny about just talking?'" Yet Denboski, certain he heard something in his discovery, convinced a friend at Chuckles, the club where comics were groomed to appear at the Laughter Lounge—both venues were owned by the same corporation, Mirthfull, Inc (sic)—to set aside five minutes for Myles on a slow night. The friend—a man named Al (his surname isn't known)—agreed, and on a Wednesday night, with closing hour very near, Myles condensed his now thirty minute routine into four and received from the drunks remaining one of his harshest rebukes. "Tell some fucking jokes, skinhead!" Still, Al saw something as well in Myles, and told him, that night, that he could have a precious fifteen minute slot in a week, but he needed to try

and "be funnier," an enigmatic direction that might have
stuck Myles in an inescapable quandary had not Lewis
Denboski interceded. Denboski said, "They want some wise
ass up there who says, 'Look at what a bunch of jackasses
you are.'" Then he handed over a pile of videotapes, which
at first created some difficulty: Myles, by no means affluent
and still working at the library, owned no VCR. But this
was solved by their watching together in Denboski's office
a series of specials featuring Sikes, Mr. Motormouth, and
others, such as Oz Paradise, King David Blum, and Dena
Cuomo, one of the era's few female comics. They regaled
with their observations and insults and profane perspectives
on modern life, leaving audiences, as was the typical phrase
of the day, "rolling in the aisles." Myles writes, "You didn't
see what was so funny. Neither did Mr. D. Each comic
seemed to steal from each other. They used obscenity like a
hammer, beating the audience until they seemed subdued
instead of charmed." After viewing three tapes, Denboski
said to Myles, "See what I mean? Come up with ten minutes
of that, throw in some impersonations, and you'll be on
your way."

Myles took home with him the tapes, and the next day at
work—he was by now a full-time desk librarian—checked
out a VCR, a bulky item he could not strap to his bike, as he
had with the film projectors; the VCR he had to carry, leaving
his bike behind to catch a bus home. After many more hours
of viewing the tapes, he could not, however, generate any
material, similar to what he'd seen or not. "Every time you
tried, your brain seemed to squeeze shut like a fist." What
he could do, though, in no time at all, was copy the things
the comics said and mimic their voices, from Oz Paradise's
breezy ramble, to Mr. Motormouth's syllable a second
patter; even Dena Cuomo's screechy whine cascaded from
his mouth as easily as breath. Come that next Wednesday,
judging by Myles's own brief account—and factoring for his
signature modesty—his fifteen minutes at Chuckles were a

huge hit. Not one remnant of what he called his "Master's Act" remained; it was all mimicry of contemporary observational comics, pitch-perfect duplicates of their—in Myles's mind—crude and mindless blather. "Afterward, Al booked you to a permanent spot, three nights a week, and offered at last to pay. The other comics, whose jokes seemed even less humorous than those of your subjects, wanted to talk to you, see how you could mimic and how long you'd been at it, but all you really wanted was to leave and visit Mr. D, to show him his confidence wasn't wasted."

Sadly, as is borne out in the manuscript and more fully in the Metro Section of the next morning's *Dispatch*, Lewis Denboski was not there to hear of his charge's success. According to the brief article's headline, on page B-6, "Longtime club owner murdered." It seems that while closing up the Giggle Room, Denboski was accosted by a pair of masked youth, and subsequently shot when he refused to go back in for the night's receipts. And while both assailants were subsequently incarcerated, and the Denboski family kept the Giggle Room open another ten years, Myles never returned. Nor did he attend the funeral. "You had been to enough of those already," he writes.

Still, he did not let this loss deter him. That he only knew Denboski a total of twenty-six days might have prevented a bond from solidifying, but what mattered most to Myles then was going forward, as he believed that's what Denboski would have wanted. "He hoped to see a revival of mimicry, and he saw you as the one who might lead audiences there." Despite his three nights weekly at Chuckles, he continued his eight- hour days at the library and viewed new videos of other comics on his free evenings. Rhino Stamps, the heckler's nightmare. King David Blum, whose rants offended and amused Jews and Gentiles with equal facility. Mandingo, one of few black observational comics, who performed bare-chested and entered and exited the stage with buxom white women on both arms.

Cousin Ezra, whose hillbilly act harked back slightly to the vernacular storytellers, though surely those gentleman would have blushed to hear Cousin Ezra's explicit accounts of adolescent urges and comely bovines. It took little time for Myles to capture cadences, detect barely auditory lisps and tics, modulate his own voice to theirs in volume and timbre. As well, he memorized their material, isolating the jokes drawing the most laughter for his now thirty minute routines. He still practiced his "Masters Act" and added to his retinue of family voices none other than Lewis Denboski's "parched and torn moan." On stage, though, there was no time for esoterica or nostalgia: the Chuckles' audience demanded the voices and wit of the national stars, probably because, as Anton Greene conjectures, "the prices at Chuckles allowed a variety of consumers to enter, have a few drinks, and even snack on deep-fried hors d'oeuvres, while the admissions alone at the theaters would have taken quite a bite out of the average citizen's paycheck." (Here, it should be stated that Greene has argued that, in this nation, comedy has served as a distraction from social inequities; thereby, he assigns comics as unwitting tools of a capitalistic elite; yet even he holds a soft spot for Myles, having seen him perform when he was thirteen, marveling at how the mimic spoke for ninety consecutive minutes without a return to his own voice.)

Whether explained by economics or entertainment, Myles's celebrity was expanding and doing so rather quickly. Other club owners—from the Comedy Casbah and Sidesplitters—plied him with offers of more sets or more money. Increasingly, at the circulation desk, he was recognized by patrons of the clubs, who could not believe someone with his talents surely earned less than they. Still, he did not leave either Chuckles or the library, as he felt both had provided for him so much, and loyalty seems a virtue he held dear all his life. (Consider that even at the height of his fame—while touring his revision of Hernandez's

"Impromptu"—he made a point of performing for free at Chuckles.) Each night he performed, though, bodies surged close to the stage, the doubters trying to locate a tiny tape player on his person or examining his neck and midsection for odd musculature. At the conclusion of these shows, promoters and managers and club owners attempted to get backstage, calling out their credentials and reasons for needing a moment of his time. Business cards fluttered around his face like large snowflakes, but he never inspected them. He rode his bike home.

Four months into his residence at Chuckles, Al, his early supporter, departed for Detroit and a larger share of a restaurant that had nothing to do with the comedy business. This put Myles in a slight lurch, as he really didn't know anyone else in management—a rather faceless and humorless crew of MBA's who depended upon Al to attract talent; Myles writes he needed only one impression to represent them, as they all spoke with the same "cash-register voice." But the series of events which would take him out of his hometown were about to commence, starting with Clayton Adams III, Therese Morton's boss, the "Man Who Never Laughed," and the article he wrote for the *Dispatch*, titled, "The Bright Voices of Comedy." Amusingly, the word "voices" pointed only to Myles, not a number of young comics (though in that town, according to Greene's meticulous research, approximately 420 men and women under thirty-five received compensation for comic appearances that year alone). Further, it lavished so much praise on Myles that some suspected Adams, who was nearing seventy, either was growing senile or had another write the article for him. Thanks to the detailed diary he kept—and its preservation by his widow, Delia—we know Adams viewed Myles perform on four consecutive nights. And while the article contains such superlatives as, "finest mimic alive," "Mr. Myles has no competitors for freshness," and "unlike any comic," the diary entries, composed in a more private prose, offer this gem: "to compare this guy to the masters [whom Adams once reviewed] is to miss the point completely. They just wanted you to laugh, and they compensated for less-than-stellar mimicry with gestures, props and exaggerations. This kid seems to attract attention away from his physical self toward the voice alone. I recognized every one right away. I couldn't keep from imagining that the people were on stage with him. His voice became every one of his subjects!"

In her formative study on the vernacular storytellers, *Yokels, Yahoos and Just Plain Folks*, the grand-dame of Comedic Studies, L.P. Chance, herself the granddaughter of "Lucky" Chance, the "king of the zingers," tells the story of how Hezekiah "Uncle Ike" Stanley, master of the farm to town narrative, clipped every positive review and stuffed them in a pillowcase he clutched at his side in bed. One still hears of comics tearing up bad notices with a ritualized fervor or claiming to never read any of them while maintaining several scrapbooks. But as Myles never betrayed any emotion or habit like anyone's, it is no surprise that he makes no mention of Adams's review in the manuscript. Nor does he discuss any reviewer, despite the fact that, until his very last performances, one can find nothing but lauds. Others were reading the *Dispatch*, though, notably the management crew of Chuckles and the Laughter Lounge, a venue lusted after by every local comic with grandiose dreams. One was guaranteed a packed house there every night of the week, and, standing room only, the Double L (as the comics called it) held five hundred. Also, one might have the good fortune of being heard by a pro or one of his representatives, as, on occasion, comics stopped by to try out new material during the late-night Improv sessions. For these and other reasons, there was little doubt that the Double L was the make or break place, the last step before a national tour, then a career of theaters that held back crowds with velvet ropes and spelled out names on the grandest marquees.

Such had happened to one Jason "Speedy" Gonzales, a Chicano comic discovered on only his second night at the Double L by the manager of Dena Cuomo. His photos were displayed prominently on the walls, serving the hopeful as a reminder that the same fortune might befall them but also spurring them into thinking that they'd better get to work. (Myles did not know Speedy well, though their paths crossed, and Speedy would say, after hearing a recording of Myles "doing" him, "He could call my mamacita asking for money with that voice. And get the dinero, too!")

It was August when management decided Myles could appear four nights a week, for five hundred dollars, at the Double L. Only five months had passed since his first night at the Hub, but the dizzying ascent affected him little or not at all. He still worked at the library full-time: "You didn't want to lose your health care." And though he bought two new suits, two shirts, ties, and a pair of black shoes, the entire wardrobe, save for the shoes, was a package deal at an outlet store for men. If his act didn't distance him enough from the rank and file comedians backstage at the Double L, his formal clothing put a wall between them, as only a few wore blazers, and then typically with jeans and sneakers. But other than the new clothes, the only significant change in habit for Myles was that now he rode the bus, the 32 Crosstown, to avoid the grime and dust that collected on his trouser cuffs when he biked.

Yet the comics, though respectful—especially after Adams's review—didn't quite know what to make of him, and all he knew of them were the patterns and tones of their speech. He writes, "Backstage was the first time you saw what could be called 'the business.' Everyone phoning agents or scribbling notes. Drinking, some drug use, much nervous smoking. All this and an atmosphere of paranoia, where everyone suspects his peers of sucking up to management for choice 'slots,' or trying to 'bite a bit.' One sallow, thin man who'd apparently been there for years would always, after he spoke, draw a circle in the air and a 'C' within it, to copyright his jokes." And, as he felt when he first viewed the tapes with Lewis Denboski, Myles didn't think anyone was particularly funny. "They were too desperate. They didn't want just the audience to laugh. They wanted their peers, the bartenders, management, people passing by on the street. You didn't think you belonged at all."

From his first evening, though, he was a success. "How could he not be?" writes Melissa Tangier, one of today's freshest Comedic Studies scholars, and a biracial woman herself. "Original act, sealed with a respected critic's approval, a far sight better looking than most of the pizza-faced goons." Myles hated the Double L, which is still standing and serving as the launching pad for the newest comics from the Buckeye State. Empty, it was—and still is—as welcoming as a sanitarium. A low and long building, it was rumored to have been initially built as a bowling alley, but a bank defaulted before the lanes were installed. Unlike at Chuckles, here smoking was allowed, which, due to the low ceilings, kept a foggy bank of smoke near the performers' heads. Myles still tried to maintain a focus on anything but individual faces, so, in that regard, the smoke made it easier to not see the crowd, though it did clog his lungs and dry out his throat. Adapting, he altered his routine: at the end of his thirty minutes, when his throat was raw, his voice raspy, he impersonated the smokers, Cuomo, Blum, and Carlo Tarantella, the up and coming Italian comic from the East. Nightly, Myles received the biggest rounds of applause but performed early enough to catch the ten-thirty run of the #32. This typically left six unhappy comics with the unenviable task of following him. His talents and the applause they fetched created in his peers a good deal of envy; however, none stole from his act, though most would have done so if they knew how or what to purloin. Peter Szok allows that mimicry was a part of many an observational comic's repertoire, albeit not of specific persons, as no one since

O'Meara had strictly been a mimic. Still, King David Blum would imitate a "typical Jew" or "Goy," and Mandingo's "tight-ass white guy/bad-ass brother" routine had secured him a Hammy, the Comics' Guild award for best routine of the year. Yet, when compared to Myles, one would think most of the imitations sounded like a comic speaking in a single "funny" voice and not reproducing upwards of sixteen in thirty minutes, as was Myles's average at the time. As Clayton Adams III said presciently in his review: "When he reaches the highest stages of comedy, no one, past, present or future, will compete with this remarkable young man."

And yet they tried. The two most notable incidents, not ironically the very ones that propelled him to the "highest stages of comedy," involved two of the most prominent comedians of the day: Rhino Stamps and King David Blum. It began in Myles's second month at the Double L, where, due to the griping of other comics, he was playing the last slot of the night before the open-mic Improvs began, then catching rides home from bartenders and waitresses, none of whom "had comic aspirations." On a Friday, he wanted to introduce five new voices into his now forty-minute set, one of which was Rhino Stamps's, whose voice he'd had a small struggle with, due to what he called, "his alternately phlegmy and nasal roar." He told no one of his plans, though if he did, undoubtedly his more thuggish peers would have failed to warn him of what was common knowledge backstage: that shortly after his performance at the Palace Theater that night, Rhino and his entourage of agent, erotic dancers, and lackeys, would be arriving. (Coincidence dogs each step of Myles's performing life, one cannot deny. However, some still ascribe to him a bewitching ability to effect reality, which, while there is no concrete evidence, certainly entertains.)

So with no idea that Rhino Stamps sat in the VIP section,

flanked by fans and drinking complimentary bottles of champagne, Myles entered the stage. As was his custom now, he simply announced, "I'm Douglas Myles," as if what he was going to do should be obvious to all in attendance. Witnesses claimed—as the encounter was written up in the *Dispatch* then put out on wire services—that Stamps took no notice at first. Though an exceedingly large man—over six feet tall and three hundred pounds—the nickname he'd gotten from Blum stemmed more from his prominent and upturned nose ("Schnoz," Blum assuredly would have said) than his considerable size. As well, his subtitle, "The Heckler's Nightmare," suggested behavior not unlike that of his massive, four legged, African namesake. Rather than dispatching the drunken calls of "You suck" with such clever retorts as, "Hey, I don't criticize your drinking," Stamps would charge off the stage at a frighteningly fast pace and pull up mere inches from the heckler, then say, "I'm a little deaf. Would you mind repeating yourself?" At the time, critics said it was for this alone that the crowds came, as Rhino's other material was pedestrian and derivative, focused on an essentialist argument about men and women and fairly crude observations about bathroom habits. The latter could be seen if the heckler, for drunkenness or courage, withstood Stamps's first assault, as after whatever response the heckler made, Rhino would rear back and bellow, "I've taken shits bigger than you." Customarily, no one found out what might be Rhino's next statement.

That night, however, as Myles progressed from Cousin Ezra's gags about tossing cow pies to Mandingo's "tight-ass white guy/bad-ass brother" debate (no easy feat: mimicry of another's imitation), Rhino suspended his drinking and silenced all around him. One wonders if the comic had any idea his voice would soon issue from the mouth of the slim young man in a slightly ill-fitting suit. He had little to say about the incident. He neither spoke to reporters or other comics in the ensuing days. In less than a year, he would be in his own hometown, Chicago, performing solely at his new club, Rhino's Jungle, where each night he and his fans enacted a version of the heckler routine to thunderous applause.

On stage, after impersonating Oz Paradise, Mr. Motormouth, and moving to the smokers, Tarantella, Cuomo and Blum, Myles launched into Rhino's male/female routine, his voice alternating perfectly between nasality and being clogged with spit as he uttered such forgettable lines as, "My girl complained I didn't take her to see any chick flicks, so I brought home a movie we'd both like. You know what it's called? Chicks Who Dig Chicks Volume Eight!" Stamps's entourage looked to their meal ticket then to the mimic, he as still and as thin as the microphone stand before him, his perfect recreation of Stamps's voice causing more laughter and applause than the original routine ever earned. Myles's final impression was, to the crowd, an obscure one, later discovered to be of Simpkins, who ended every show with the lines Myles spoke that night: "All of us have a story to tell, but some of us have a lot of voices to tell it with. Thank you for listening to mine." A curious reference to his "Masters Act," to be sure, but as well a sign of what was next to come in his career, the wonderfully dense "History Lesson." Yet even if any in the audience had heard of Simpkins, they wouldn't have paid attention, as Rhino Stamps, at full gait, was lumbering toward the stage. Witnesses nearby said they could feel every reverberation of his feet thumping the floor. None, though, saw any fear betrayed in Myles's features. He wrote nothing about this incident, unless one considers the following sentence: "You made enemies, but not intentionally." That night, while he saluted the crowd, he started to exit, then paused. He turned around as Rhino Stamps was landing on the stage, then leapt forward to meet him nose to nose, behind the microphone stand, and actually beat Rhino by a few seconds in saying, "I'm a little deaf. Would you mind repeating what you said?"

Most gasped, but some laughed, chalking up, as one witness said, "the first round to Myles." Stamps stepped back, as if his opponent weighed more than one-sixty-five in hard soled shoes, then composed himself by hiking up his trousers and sneering to the audience. He opened his mouth in time to hear his voice say, "I've taken bigger shits than you," but his lips hadn't moved. The speaker, of course, was Myles, and the audience response was total: a standing ovation with applause, whistles and praise so rich, a bartender said, "You'd think no one had ever heard a joke before." Once the jubilant wave of noise had crested, Myles offered his hand to Stamps, who, shoulders slumped, exited the stage.

The coverage occasioned by this triumph took the name of Douglas Myles, for the first time, beyond his hometown, into the larger world of professional comedy. The story was repeated in entertainment pages of newspapers, discussed on morning radio programs. He sat for a photographer's portrait—his first since his senior year of high school—for a planned cover of *The Jester*, the still-thriving monthly magazine chronicling comedy in all its permutations. The cover was to pair his image with Stamps's, but it never went to press, as things were happening so quickly, the never materialized feud between these principals was surpassed by event of even greater import.

For within two weeks of the encounter with Stamps, Myles would receive a call from the producers of the *H.H. McCormick Show*, an hour-long program that featured equal parts politicians, sports figures, actors and comics, in a simple format: the towheaded Manhattanite, H.H. McCormick, wearing horn rim glasses and polka dot bow ties, talking with guests before live audiences. Said Carlo Tarantella, only three months distant from his second appearance, "You could tour the best theaters year round and not get as much buzz as fifteen minutes with McCormick." On learning of

Myles's invitation, the Double L's management team were beside themselves to have another of "their boys" ascend to that level, especially since it had been three years since Speedy Gonzales's debut on the *McCormick Show*. They prepped Myles on how to dress, telling him to eschew his stage wear for an open collar so he would look less "uptight." One suggested spectacles. Another mentioned he'd look more forceful with a goatee. All demanded he mention the name of the Laughter Lounge as many times as he could. As for the comics he was leaving behind, only a handful of whom would attain anything like regional or local celebrity—hosting late-night movie shows, appearing at street fairs, opening malls with bikini clad beauty queens— they did prepare, on the night of his last performance, the classic ritual of shaving cream pies on paper plates and cans of silly string, only to learn he had been collared by the management team for another prep session.

His appearance, scheduled for a Friday, required he fly, a first for the twenty-one year old, whose only experience with mass transit, other than bus rides, was a train trip to see his Aunt Glendora, a woman who lived in Philadelphia and spoke with a "slow, sputtering hiss." Nervous on the day of the flight, he was picked up by a driver hired by the Double L management, and he wore his old suit with a new tie. About wardrobe he'd decided to ignore the cash register voices, though he'd assured them he would mention the club at every opportunity. Aboard the plane, he was not recognized, and he sat bolt upright in coach from gate to gate, refusing all meals and beverages save for a bottle of water he'd brought on board. He writes, "You could say it was from the flight, but that wouldn't be true. You were fearful of leaving the Laughter Lounge for a Manhattan audience and the millions watching. You were prepared to be sent back quickly to the silos and cornfields of home."

Understandable, to say the least, is this fear, especially

when one considers how close he was to attaining fame of
which he'd never dreamed. Peter Szok asserts, "The real
surprise, considering he'd been performing for only six
months, two of them professionally, is that he even got
on the plane." But, as it turns out, his fear was warranted,
not because he'd face for the first time a television
audience—presumably more sophisticated than the folk of
his hometown—but because he had not been told by the
producers that he'd be sharing the stage with another comic,
none other than King David Blum, making his sixteenth
appearance—a record for comedians and only two less than
a senior senator from the Empire State (once considered, due
to his voting record, quite the comic himself). As inter-office
memos show, Blum, a law school graduate who'd earned
millions through a carefully managed stock portfolio, was
contacted first by the producers, and, in an interesting move,
considering his reputation, Blum forewent his thousand-
dollar appearance fee. (Myles received five hundred.) All
evidence points to the production staff seeking a rancorous
thirty minutes (which would become a full fifty, bumping
retired rear admiral Elliot Alcorn to discuss his new book
the next night). They sought squabble, clamor, if not outright
evisceration, pitting the novice against the seven-time comic
of the year. To make matters worse for Myles, Blum sought
vengeance, as it was well known among insiders (Myles,
a novice, black, and a Buckeye, couldn't have been more
outside) that Blum harbored a special affection for Stamps,
the uncertified rumor being Stamps had once served ably
as Blum's bodyguard. To most, this made sense, as Blum's
press releases always alleged his self-dubbed "toxic material
made as many enemies as it did fans." As well, there was
his naming of Rhino, and their many appearances together
on tour and television. About Blum, Myles said, in the
interview before the ambush, that he was "easily one of
the best," though in the manuscript, he writes, "What you
could never understand about Blum, after you discovered

the lachrymose quality beneath his insults and the emphasis he put on second syllables, was whether he believed in anything he said."

As a surprise guest, Blum was not backstage when Myles arrived, spirited to the studio by a driver and now feeling everyone could detect his provincial background "like manure on your soles." He balked at makeup, asking the artist if the foundation were designed for whites. Nodding, she prepared to smear his face, but he ducked, saying, "I want to look like me." Glassy-eyed, he stared at the intricate workings of backstage while steered by an aide to the Green room. The schedule he received (found in the same accordion file as the manuscript) detailed that he'd appear with McCormick for fifteen minutes, then get ten for his act, which, strangely, he'd already decided would be absent of a Blum impression, as he'd selected comics whose best jokes could be repeated over public broadcast. Mr. Motormouth, Mandingo, and Dena Cuomo would be his subjects, Carlo Tarantella if he had time left. (Though this is only known from his telling it to a production aide who asked. It should be noted that Myles on occasion diverted from the plans he shared backstage, one notorious case being his first performance of Hernandez's "Impromptu," on a night he claimed he'd do an abbreviated "History Lesson.") However, the schedule was false, as he'd only get ten minutes with McCormick before Blum would "bust in," as one producer wrote in a memo, "and tear this kid a new one."

Though the first few minutes of the interview are only a prelude to what the producers—McCormick was in on it, too—planned as their "main event," it is interesting to view those questions and their halting but thorough replies. He mainly discusses gigs in his hometown but when McCormick asked about his background, Myles is careful to say, for what is likely the first time in public, "I'm black."

"Really," a bemused McCormick says, shuffling through

his index cards. "I never would have guessed."

Myles, who appears washed out and sickly with his lack of makeup, nods at this and says in a voice as artificially comic as those of the one-liner royalty, "If I had a dollar for every time I heard that." He then tells of his performance before Rhino Stamps and his act in general (mentioning twice the Double L), his inflection even, his hands locked on his knees. The audience is strangely silent, laughing little, for once finding humor in McCormick's asides—his stale jokes usually elicited groans. An assistant producer, later on, would say that in the production booth the staff began to openly pity the young man, as in person he seemed far more defenseless against Blum's imminent assault. But they could do nothing, as McCormick was reading the last question, the cue for Blum: "Is there anyone you can't do?"

After a silence of seconds, Myles licked his lips, and, in the "reedy Yankee lockjaw" of McCormick, repeated the question. No applause sounded, but if one looks carefully at the video, one can see it was not due to disapproval but to shock, as the faces appear as blank as slate, and not a few fans clasp hands over open mouths. One must slow the video's speed to detect this, as, in seconds, the camera shifts to King David Blum, smoking a cigarette, bounding past McCormick and standing before the audience, his arms lifted, palms open, as the audience, to a man, stands and claps with a zeal like that heard in Pentecostal churches. Blum, who was forty at the time and handsome as a matinee idol, if a little gray, makes a point of shaking McCormick's hand, then stares, arms folded across his chest, at Myles, who gamely offers his trembling hand. At this point, Blum spits out the cigarette and stomps on it. He jabs an index finger at Myles and shouts, "You ready, punk?"

As the crowd begins to roar lustily, the show cuts to commercial. If the overt staginess of the first segment is not evident, the image displayed on the return to taping is obvious: a split screen of Blum and Myles with the legend

"Tale of the Tape" below their chins. After a bell's tolling, the show's announcer, Jack Walker (himself a mildly successful former social critic) intones the ages, weights and heights of each man, concluding with their "records": Myles, one and oh; Blum, "never been beaten." As well as this played with the audience and the viewers (the ratings share grew steadily over the course of the evening until it seemed every TV household tuned in), critics, the next day, saw this as a reason to take the *H.H. McCormick Show* to task. "No way," wrote a reviewer in the *Post*, "the production staff could have done this off the cuff. They set that kid up." Yet, as every critic would mention, their initial disdain for the show and sympathy for "that kid" was on its way to a sudden transformation.

But for a full fifteen minutes, Blum dominated, subsequent to McCormick's question: "Have you seen his act?"

Stalking the small stage, playing to the crowd, Blum said, "No, but I've heard about it." Knowing Blum, the staff had shifted to a seven-second delay to censor him. (Blum, a veteran of the show, likely expected this.) While the transcript expurgates all the obscenities, the video itself captures them all. There's no need, however, to repeat each one, nor is there need to reproduce the entire monologue, for, as Owen Delaney, the editor of The Jester, summed up in his column: "He essentially said, in a variety of ways, with enough blue words to make a sailor blush, that Myles wasn't funny and he had no material of his own."

Considering his very attempts, at Al and Lewis Denboski's behest, it seems Myles might have agreed with that accusation in part, but in the next segment, titled "Round Two"—the first round scored as Blum's—Myles, finally given an opportunity to speak, quietly says, without any joking, "My favorite of the masters was Arthur Simpkins. And he always tried, in his act, to provide variety. He had a set number of voices, but he was always adding or changing the order. And I think from him I've seen how you can keep things fresh, rather than saying the same thing over and over again."

McCormick taps his cards against his desk, the audience murmurs, and Blum fires up a new cigarette, then blows the smoke at Myles. He says, "Listen, I'm no Rhino Stamps. I love the big ape, but you're not going to make me look like a yutz. I know your little fucking plan, kid. I know you're going to mimic me, and feel free, I've got a funny voice, I talk like a Jew, or maybe you call us Yids back where you come from, or Kike, or Heb, whatever. But talking like me won't shut me up. Just try, just try." The camera is tight on his long, sweating face until another commercial comes on. Remaining in the program are twenty-five minutes, excluding station breaks, and upon the return to the show, the score is two rounds to zero for Blum, another signal, according to Hector Cruz, the famous critic from the *Times*, that the show's producers were biased toward Blum, as, "If anything, with Blum's uninventive bluster . . . and Myles's intriguing and calm reply, that 'round' should have been scored a draw."

Here, though, despite its "expletives deleted," is where the show's transcript best illustrates the performances, as the video, complicated by swift cuts and blurry focus, makes for vertiginous viewing. After another salvo from Blum, in which for two minutes, with deliberate, football-cheer syllables, he chanted, "Not Funny," McCormick steps in:

McCormick: What do you have to say to that, Mr. Myles?

Myles (in own voice): Repetition isn't truth.

McCormick (shaking his head): Care to elaborate?

Blum (walking by, blowing smoke): He's scared. I've taken away his one (expletive deleted) joke, that's not even a (e.d.) joke in the first (e.d.) place. He can't copy me, the little pisher, so he just mumbles.

Myles (in own voice): I meant that saying something

many times doesn't make it true.

Blum: Then say something funny! Prove me wrong. I bet this yutz couldn't even tell a (e.d.) knock-knock joke without (e.d.) it up.

McCormick (tugging ends of tie): You really haven't said anything like a joke. Care to share one?

Myles (in Blum's voice): Then the Jewish kid says, "Of course your priest's a genius, you guys tell him everything."

(Audience gasps and laughter)

Blum: I haven't told that one since my (e.d.) mitzvah.

Myles (in own voice): You have told it before.

Blum (turning to McCormick): Mac, don't you see. This is my point, exactly.

Myles (eyes closed, in Blum's voice): Mac, don't you see…

Blum: Shut the (e.d.) up. Jesus. That's all he can do. What are you, some kind of freak? I had a cousin, named Arnie, he…

Myles (interrupting, in Blum's voice): Had this photographic memory. Trouble was, he stuttered.

Blum: So you know my old (e.d.). So (e.d.) what? Any slob with a record player remembers that bit.

Myles (in Blum's voice): And by the time he'd, duh-duh-duh-duh, s-s-s-say wh-what was on his muh-muh-mind…

Blum: Jesus, are you even listening? Hello? (Waves hand across Myles's face.) Anyone home?

(Audience laughter)

Myles (in own voice): You're right. That bit isn't funny.

McCormick (over crowd noise, fanning himself with cards): Ouch, hey, we'll be right back.

Blum: Don't break for commercial! Don't you (e.d.) dare. I (e.d.) made this (e.d.) show! You (e.d.) owe me. Don't (e.d.) with the King. They call me the King . . .

Myles (in Blum's voice): Because anyone who messes

with me, Jew, Gentile, Black, Asian, even the noble Native, anyone who messes with me gets crowned. Boom!

(Standing Ovation)

Blum (facing the audience): But that's mine, don't you get it? You're laughing at a trick, a gimmick, not what he says. Jesus, you're all a bunch of, a bunch of . . .

Myles (in Blum's voice): A bunch of hyenas, you'll laugh at anything today.

Blum: That one I've never said, putz. You got it all wrong.

Myles (in own voice): But you will say it next week.

At this point, Blum says nothing. He doesn't even open his mouth. The audience mumbles and moans in the way that usually attends an unanswered schoolyard challenge. When the taping resumes, Blum is no longer on stage. McCormick and Myles shake hands, McCormick apologizes to the rear admiral and promises as entertaining a show tomorrow. The applause deafens.

Had any other comedian been enlisted to provide Myles's comeuppance, the last line of their exchange might have eventually faltered, as most, when surveyed by The Jester, replied that they'd have avoided the stage for a week, allowing the public to forget Myles's prediction (our national attention span as short as it is). But King David Blum was not called king for nothing. Few had a mild response to his act, so he was met at every concert by fans and detractors alike, all of them now turning out to see if the upstart from, as Blum called it, "the fucking prairie," knew more than the comic's voice and routine, but as well the workings of his mind. In the manuscript, Myles writes briefly about his return home and the party at the Double L (he left early to catch his bus), and the attention he received from the local media. No mention, however, of Blum, who was defiant toward every reporter who asked him if he were at all worried or if he felt the contest, as scored by most critics, was a majority decision for Myles. "Those hacks," he said in Des Moines. "They're all a bunch of would-be comics, but they didn't have the chutzpah or the talent. They've been after me for years." A night later, in Lake Charles, at their famous outdoor amphitheater built in the shape of an oyster shell, he told the crowd, "I don't know what show they were watching, but all I remember was him stuttering and shifting his eyes. He needed to duck, because I was shooting with both barrels." (Never mind that the stammering was from his act, King David had his reply.) Then, in Houston, during a radio interview: "Everybody comes after the big guy. That's what I did when social critics were top dogs. I took out Finkel and 'Streetfighter' Archibald on an episode of Archibald's show. Now? I'm still standing. I don't know where whatshisname is." On the eve of a week's passing, in El Paso, at the Rodeo Pavilion, he said, "Clock's ticking. The day I rely on Mr. Xerox for material, that's the day I hang it up."

For those present the next night in Albuquerque, at a brand new theater called the Rialto, the night was a curious one, filled with deep blue skies, distant thunder and flashes of heat lightning. Apparently, Blum's afternoon nap—he would complain the next day—had gone longer than he'd expected, as a desk clerk at the hotel forgot to place a wake up call. As a result, Blum arrived at the Rialto logy and late, as well as suffering, he later declared, from a slight head cold. The pins and needles of his twenty-four-hour medication hadn't dulled when he entered the stage to a packed house. The biggest distraction of all, though, came from a certain patron, seated somewhere near the front, toward Blum's right, who kept saying, "Do the 'Photographic Memory' routine from 'Dirty Mind.'" Until his death—and it's worth noting that Blum performed until lung cancer silenced him permanently at the age of sixty-one—until then, he insisted that this concertgoer and the hotel desk clerk were in Myles's employ. "Just like the fraud Hernandez," he'd rail, somewhat inaccurately. "The guy even copies his sabotage." What is certain is that thirty minutes into the show, Blum, sweating more than usual, looking grayer, paused in the middle of his classic routine about goys at a seder—"Do what with the crackers?"—and addressed the man: "My Christ, you're persistent. That bit's older than the hair on your balls. Jesus. You people. You're like. Well, you know what you are is." And before he could blink, he finished what Myles said he would, and for perhaps the first time ever at a King David Blum show, neither the spectators nor the performer had anything to say.

At this point, suspicions began to surface, suggesting Myles's were more than the powers to execute pitch-perfect mimicry, that he possessed some kind of psychic ability as well. Around his hometown, since his first appearance, people surmised that his mimicry was too good to be the result of practice, and they guessed at the black arts or demonic possession as explanations. Now, though, the speculation was taking place on a national scale, in tandem with the demands that the rising star display his talents, whatever their source, on stages trod by King David and his ilk, along with Banks, O'Meara, and Salvatore, many years before.

He accepted the offers, finally finding in the lucrative future a reason to stop working at the library. "You were never happy as a shelver," he writes. "Or as a stamper. But when it was time to go, it was a hard job to give up. It was the only one you'd ever had." Still, he had little time to reflect over this, as there was much planning to do. Though courted by a number of prospects—especially individual members of the management team of Chuckles and the Laughter Lounge—he did not select a manager. The person who made the arrangements and set the dates, during the whole of his career, was always Myles alone. Greene, ever the adherent of class and economics, asserts at the time that comics didn't need management, as they were mostly from middle- to upper-class backgrounds, a claim supported by the observations of Lamar Jackson, a protégé of Mandingo's and the comic closest to Myles. At this time, Jackson was still playing clubs like Chuckles, but going against type with a nerd act. Much later, he would tell Greene, "No one had to have an agent, really. King David didn't, Mr. Motormouth and Dena Cuomo didn't, and none of them ended up in the poorhouse. If you had stocks and mutual funds, you handed them over to a good broker. An accountant took care of your taxes. Most of us were college grads. Putting together a fifty state tour wasn't the logistical nightmare the fans might imagine."

On his own, Myles established an appearance fee—1,500 a night (two thousand less than Blum, a thousand less than Rhino Stamps). He arranged his performances and paid for plane tickets and accommodations with a newly acquired credit card. (A model customer, he always paid off balances in a timely manner.) He writes: "You could sit at your new table in the house and plan out an entire year if you wanted. Dates and hotel rooms and flights were like pieces to an elaborate but interesting puzzle." His first tour was of clubs like the Double L, and he played one hundred and seventeen in two hundred days, building on the foundation of his *H.H. McCormick Show* success, and earning the respect of his fellows. Carlo Tarantella, who saw him for the first time in a Boston club called Merrymakers, suggested, "When he does my pasta jokes, I think he tells them funnier." This sentiment was echoed by Mr. Motormouth, who told a Denver reviewer, "I hear my stuff, my stuff now, coming out of his mouth, and it's like I'm hearing it for the first time." Yet for all the press accolades and the burgeoning professional acceptance, no critic, and no performer, save for Jackson—and this would come later—could cite a budding friend- or acquaintanceship; they all were, in the words of

Dena Cuomo, "afraid he'd only imitate us better if we hung out with him." Not that Myles reached out much either: as was his custom at his hometown's clubs, he left as soon as he finished his act, stopping backstage perhaps to drink a bottle of water. Then he'd catch a cab to his hotel, and, judging by his credit card receipts (all of which he scrupulously kept in the same accordion file as his tax records and the manuscript), his most extravagant purchases would be a room service pizza. No affairs with models, actresses, or even the very willing camp-followers—rim-shots, they were called, because, "if they came," said Oz Paradise, "it was after the comic." Simply put: an arrival, an appearance in his gray, black or blue suit, then two hours of unbelievably fine mimicry, followed by an exit as unceremonious as his entrance.

But it simplifies matters too much to say Myles was devoted, single-mindedly, to performing. One thing that does stand out in many accounts of that first tour is his interest in reaching out to the black community—often overlooked or forgotten by more than just the comics. To the owners of the clubs, who sent invitations to prominent local reviewers, he'd request they contact members of the black press; in fact, all of the cities he played at during that tour (and those subsequent) had flourishing black or minority newspapers, in which one finds positively glowing reviews of Myles's shows. He'd also frequently ask black bartenders and waitresses where he might get his hair cut or where he could get some real soul food. And while he details no specific visits, he writes two revealing items. "When you walked among people in these parts of town, few stared. You felt more welcome there than you'd felt in a while." As well, though, he writes: "You told a national audience you were black and still people with two drinks in them asked if you were Greek or Jordanian. And often were disappointed when you said no."

During the performances, though, Myles revealed

nothing about himself. He only spoke in his own voice
for the introduction—"I'm Douglas Myles"—and the
conclusion—"Thanks"—and a brief prelude to his "Masters
Act," which he was increasingly slipping in between what
he was calling then the "Contemporary Scene." Partly, this
points to the development of the "History Lesson"—a two-
and-a-half hour journey from the one-liner royalty, all the
way up to his peers. As well, what he said precisely points
to a deep kinship with the virtually forgotten Simpkins. (At
the time, following L.P. Chance's lead, articles appeared
about Banks, Salvatore, O'Meara and Hernandez, but essays
on Simpkins didn't appear until Myles called attention to
him.) Each night he alluded to all of the greats, singling out
Simpkins as the one he liked best, but on his last night, in
the Jubilee Station of New Orleans, he said, "I never saw
him perform, of course. Most of you don't even know his
name. But without him, I don't think I'd have a reason to be
here."

   After three months of rest, Myles was ready to tour again,
this time premiering the "History Lesson." In it, he devoted
a good portion of time impersonating Simpkins, perhaps
spending more time with the "stammering affectations" of
his voice than any other comic. But he'd begin with the one-
liner royalty—so named because they all had some regal
honorific: Lucky Chance, "King of the Zingers," Morris
"Prince of Putdowns" Gold and Ivan "the Duke of Droll"
Roth. Their jokes referred not to politics or cultural matters
but to expensive or ineffective doctors, women drivers,
henpecked husbands, and they relied heavily on schoolboy
double-entendres that had first entertained resort patrons,
then the nation, when transmitted over the radio in the days
before television's advent. Most of these comics had gotten
their start on Happy McGowan's "Happy Hour." McGowan,
a ventriloquist, was famed for owning six different dummies,
all of them intricately designed with individual expressions
and different outfits, ranging from sailor suits to buckskin,

overalls, the like, yet the voice he threw for all of them (badly, most thought), sounded no different from his own, a "foggy tenor" Myles devoted a few minutes to, as he'd done with Sam Mack in the "Masters Act."

From the one-liner royalty, he moved to the vernacular storytellers: the aforementioned Uncle Ike among them, along with Daffy Dan Dukes, Sheriff Hogbottom, and Moonshine Jones, the legendary drunk act who earned such praise as, "Even his mock-eructations come with a southern accent." Of the periods he recreated with his voice alone—no costumes, no backdrops, no music changes—the storytellers and their artificially rustic tales gave him the easiest time, as, he writes, "all of them spoke in slight variations of the same fluctuating, nasal twang that no one from the Bluegrass or Volunteer state has ever uttered." (A perceptive comment, this: current research reveals most of the great storytellers grew up outside of Appalachia, including Jones, born and bred in Philadelphia.)

From these, he offered his beloved Masters, the longest period of the show, and the most celebrated by older critics like Clayton Adams III, who flaunted to his peers his being the first to tag the newest comic genius. (During the one time they met, a moment captured by a *Dispatch* photographer, little more was said than, "Wonderful show" and "Thanks." In the photo, Adams beams as the two shake hands, while Myles looks out in space, his face, Melissa Tangier describes, "as tight as that of a man next in line for a vaccination.") One could sense, it has been written, his reverence for all when he "did" Simpkins, O'Meara, Banks, Salvatore and Hernandez, though with the latter two, he spent the least time, noting, "You didn't like repeating broken English. You feared it might offend."

Then, without so much as a drink of water or a return to his own voice, he maneuvered his way into the tart tongues of the social critics, they who removed the sheen from the mimics and who paved the way for the observational comics. Some reviewers detected his approximations of these comics made for the only point at which he twisted or manipulated voices in a way that lampooned the comics themselves, as if in reprisal for the damage they'd done to the art of mimicry. Here one might recall his lament of feeling "born at the wrong time," but, then again, the inflections and patterns and voices he duplicated were themselves a strange ensemble. Seth Finkel, who assaulted the middle classes with a trumpeting baritone that sounded like an obscure impression itself. The sole black comic of the day, Milton Love, who, according to his biographer, patterned his speech after a famed British actor, in order to juxtapose it against his "street lingo," which initially upset traditional comedy crowds but gradually became as familiar as the diet soft drinks he later endorsed, in particular his catch phrase of, "If the shoe fits, wear it." And, of course, no treatment of this period, as Myles fully knew, could be complete without Ray "Streetfighter" Archibald, who, as his genuine inner city roots would suggest (Love and Finkel, ironically, were born in neighboring bedroom communities of Washington, D.C.), began with the sharpest fangs, and he flashed them at every one, the rich, poor, Protestant, Catholic, urban and rural, immigrant and native; but eventually he allowed success to dull them, as could be seen when he hosted a TV program called Where It's At that ridiculed relentlessly but often betrayed a mainstream conservative bent. Myles concluded this part of the "History Lesson" by capturing perfectly the harsh, almost violent tone of Archibald's early years ("a megaphone with an ax to grind") to the blunted syllables he emitted to the TV camera.

At long last, he'd arrive at the contemporaries. And though fans howled and pleaded, Myles conspicuously dropped King David Blum and Rhino Stamps. (Out of charity, some argue; others contend he didn't think much of them.) Instead, he breezed through Mandingo, Dena Cuomo, Tarentella, and some of the newer performers, such as Lamar Jackson and Speedy Gonzales. This was, however, the section of the act that allowed for the most variations. The order was never the same: one night he'd perform Mr. Motormouth's trademark spiel about the condoms available at drug stores along with Cousin Ezra's paean to "stepsister lovin'," only to drop both from the act the next evening and include Lamar Jackson's bit on attending night school to learn how to speak better Black English—"I be, She be, We all be." No matter whom he impersonated, though, and in what order, one could anticipate an impressive array of different contemporary voices, and in the words of Dena Cuomo, "If you closed your eyes, you'd think the whole Comics' Guild was up there."

Today, scholars debate whether the "History Lesson" represents the apogee of Myles's professional accomplishment. Some, like Szok, look to his earlier days, while others, Melissa Tangier among them, maintain that the best was yet to come with his resurrection and improvement of Hernandez's "Impromptu." Most, however, point to the "History Lesson," in its diversity, quality and gravity—it was, Greene insists, a lesson, after all—as not only Myles's standard of comparison but also that for all comics who have followed him. At the time, critics were unanimous in their praise, for whether they were of Clayton Adams III's generation, or similar in age to Hector Cruz, or as new to their field as Myles had been to his: all found material to respect, admire, and, as Rex Humphrey, the nineteen-year-old reviewer for his university paper, put it, "wet your pants over." Myles's own peers displayed a general approbation, yet some feared he might render them obsolete. Mr. Motormouth, in his ninth year of national tours, bemoaned, "Who needs the real me, when everyone prefers Myles's version?" But this complaint was neither serious or true (exaggeration, one should remember, is often the observational comic's preferred trope), as seen by the amount of money spent by the average household, on comedy records, video tapes, and concert tickets per week: thirty five dollars and ninety-one cents, according to Greene's stellar research team. At nearly twice that spent on music, film, theater and only ten dollars less than all sports combined, it stands to reason that not every citizen was stuffing her disposable income in Myles's coffers. "Few comics ... went hungry," Greene pithily sums up.

Moreover, the "History Lesson" was not, from its first performance at Chuckles, wholly embraced by the comic audience. During that late night open mic Improv session, an unbilled Myles stunned the crowd with an abbreviated version. Initially, though, laughter was sparse, but it gradually picked up, particularly when he turned the corner from mimics to social critics. He would go on to write, "You began to wish for more diverse audiences. You'd always hoped there were blacks and other minorities (though you never really saw who was out there), but now you wanted older people, students and professors, activists and the like. Anything but a house filled with those who cut their teeth on social critics or grew up with nothing but the numbing observations of your peers." (It should be said that Myles never publicly criticized anyone—unless one considers his barbs on the *H.H. McCormick Show*—despite being given ample opportunities. His standard reply to the question, "What do you really think about today's comics?" was, "There's certainly a lot of talent today.")

During the tour that followed, a year long affair, performed entirely in plushly carpeted theaters with orchestra pits, balconies and private loges, he was not met by the audience he was wishing for, even though he made certain that promotional materials and ads appeared in places comics usually overlooked: senior citizen centers, elite universities, free weekly newspapers and public access cable. As well, he did more radio promotion than he would ever do. No interviews, but several five-minute presentations, in his own voice, exhorting people of all walks of life to attend. His appearance fee had gone up to 2500 dollars, five hundred of which he promised would go to the charity that sent the most representatives to his show. (Later, he'd amend that to five hundred dollars and the cost of their tickets, a move that nearly ate up his entire appearance fee one night in Memphis, when over two hundred members of the Shelby County Literacy Project turned out.) Records show he played to nothing but SRO crowds, three nights a week, sometimes two shows a night, but the seats, aisles, and lobbies were filled with people his age for the most part, who coughed and clapped politely until they heard the "screechy whine" of Dena Cuomo or Lamar Jackson's "asthmatic wheeze." The critical response should have cheered him, but according to Jackson, who warmed up for Myles in several cities—in which, out of respect, Myles would not mimic him—the only parts of the newspaper Myles ever read were the front page and the business section, never turning to the entertainment supplements where critics praised daily his genius, depth and range. "He never smiled," Jackson said. "Even when he was getting a standing O." As it should be, when possible, Myles's is the last word on the tour: "They endured the first hour, maybe the first hour and a half. They choked down their vegetables in order to get two big servings of dessert."

The tour complete, he took a year off, in part to "rest his voice," he told Clayton Adams III over the phone. (Six months after reporting this, Adams retired from his post, then shortly after succumbed to a battle with pneumonia. Myles was invited to the funeral—an invitation was found among his papers; as was his custom, he sent flowers in reply, along with a donation to Adams's preferred charity, but he did not attend the service or internment.) He bought a house in a racially mixed neighborhood nearer the comedy clubs, and went on vacations to England and Ireland (his father's ancestral homes) and a railroad tour of the South. But he did not, as he would in the future, disappear entirely from the scene, nor did he remain completely silent. The unauthorized biographies characterize him during this period as aloof, alien, and often not heard from for months—the better to suggest his strangeness, if not his need to channel spirits or commune with devils—yet he could be very social, especially among the families in the neighborhoods around his new home (presently a shrine visited, along with the library, the Double L, and Chuckles, year round). Many of the neighborhood children—now adults with families of their own—remember him buying lemonade from their stands, and seeing him riding his bike to and from the market. Some recall he was eager to talk with anyone, as long as the subject was not his fame.

Nor was he maladroit as a businessman; he knew too much time away could remove his name from the public imagination, and there were new comics emerging, Jennifer Gean and Mindy Deskins among them, young Anglo women who cursed as often and creatively as David Blum while expressing a sexuality that made the earthy Dena Cuomo gasp. To stay visible, he visited Chuckles and the Double L during his first six months off. Applause always followed his entrances and exits, as did urgings that bordered on the frantic for him to perform. To this request, he'd say in Carlo Tarantella's "bristly and booming caw" of a voice, "I'm just here to watch … and bite some bits!" Perhaps twice he treated crowds to a few voices from his "Contemporary Scene" act, but never for so long as to dominate or obscure the performers there struggling to make their name. Most often, he sat near the stage, instead of the VIP section, signing autographs, drinking spring water. In the words of Jason "Cuddles" Wilkes—a three hundred pound up and comer who greeted crowds with, "Can you see me back there?"—Myles looked on "like a man trying to find the rest rooms."

Further, he issued a record, a live taping of the "History

Lesson" from a show in Miami's Coastal Palm Theater. As
long as the routine was—exceeding most comic routines by
forty minutes to an hour—it was released as a two record set,
the first of its kind. Still, at the time of its release, few stores
could keep it in stock long, though Myles had suspicions:
"You wondered if anyone listened to the whole thing."
Despite this concern, the record stayed at number one well
into the next year, by the time he was performing again. To
show its endurance, one need only look at its sales history:
it has never gone out of print, and, according to its label, still
sells approximately ten thousand copies a year. (Melissa
Tangier affirms it is perhaps the comedy record most likely
to be played at 16 RPM, as neophytes attempt to "capture
his secrets.") As well, the "History Lesson" was recently
named comic album of the century, topping Blum's "Dirty
Mind" and "Streetfighter" Archibald's "Laugh Riot." Yet, as
important as it is to mention its successes, it is interesting to
note its curiosities: for one, no photograph of Myles appears
on the cover. On the front is a collage of comics' faces:
Simpkins is featured in the center foreground, flanked by
O'Meara and Hernandez, with photos of Moonshine Jones,
Happy McGowan, Martin Love above them, and, at the
top, photos of Mr. Motormouth, Mandingo and Cuomo.
The rear cover features an audience shot, row upon row of
faces, some looking stunned, most split wide with laughter.
No liner notes appear anywhere on the inside, only the title
again and the segments, broken down into times, with the
names of the impersonated comics listed beneath. Scholars
now ponder if the absence of "personality" displayed
here—in addition, Myles's own voice isn't heard—signals
the disappearance of his own sense of self, but Tangier
dismisses this as mostly speculation, not too far from "the
kind of gossip traded in by his early biographers." However,
all agree that there is something to be said about the fact
that Myles apparently did not own a copy of the album.

"You didn't really see a need for it," he writes.

But in the first six months of his year off, he did even more. He attended the premiere on the West Coast of a biopic of O'Meara. A terrible flop that only earned back its cost through overseas distribution, it surely tried to take advantage of the mood created by Myles's "History Lesson," but, due to O'Meara's own sad life, it barely rises above bathos, as can be seen in the title, *Death of a Clown*. Still, Myles presumably sat through it, and he emerged, alone as always, holding up his hands to fans and reporters. Someone asked how he liked the picture, and he showed a thumbs-up, an image caught on tape and used by the filmmakers in a commercial touting the film's appreciation.

After the premiere, he stayed in the Golden State long enough to attend the televised awards presentation of the Comics' Guild—a union he donated money to for the establishment of pensions but never joined. Shockingly, as most critics claimed, he lost Comic of the Year to Oz Paradise, who had been, it must be said, runner up to King David Blum for five consecutive years. And while some writers contended professional jealousy and conspiracy among the voters, Myles reacted not at all. In fact, the videotape of the program shows him, at the announcement of Paradise's victory, looking relieved, as if, Melissa Tangier has written, "He feared going up on stage with only his own voice."

About his return home from the West, he'd later write: "You spent the next six months being ordinary. You shopped for groceries, cut your grass, watched baseball on TV and fell asleep no later than ten each night." He was, safe to say, far from the world of comics and comedy, but nothing in his writing or anywhere else suggests he was at all antsy or missing the adoration guaranteed him had he dressed in one of his suits and walked on stage. In the second half of his year off, his appearances at clubs grew fewer. Some speculate he considered retiring, but there is no mention of this in the manuscript, and the only "evidence" of this is a letter, purportedly typed by Myles, where he remarks fatigue and a desire to escape "the prison house of celebrity." Neither is that metaphor in keeping with his mostly straightforward prose, nor is the owner of the letter, a woman named Foster, reputable. (As well, there is some doubt he ever owned a typewriter!) Shortly after he debuted his version of the "Impromptu," she assured all that her Scandinavian-looking daughter was her and the mimic's love child—an allegation so preposterous, at the time of this writing, no agency has attempted to verify it. When he eventually emerged, twelve months and eighteen days after his last performance of the "History Lesson," he looked fitter, his hair had grown—as he could now, if he chose, afford a barber. And at the benefit performance that lured him East, he seemed more familiar with those who to his face called themselves his peers.

Again we find a time when Myles should not have been at ease among his contemporaries. Shortly after the hubbub over Oz Paradise's victory ebbed, it was whispered by comics to reporters—and always after assurances that no names would appear in any articles—that the reason Myles had not won, was in part, payback for his destruction of King David Blum, who was last seen playing, as Szok puts it, "the comic's equivalent of the second to last hurrah: the state fair circuit." Additionally, comics were jealous of Myles, not for his talent, rather, for his rapid success. Years later, Lamar Jackson would reveal, "Here was this guy, what was he back then? 21? 22? A lot of people felt he needed a bit more struggle in his life, and they were happy to supply him a little." The irony should not be lost, though one wishes Jackson had said this earlier, before all the comics of that era passed on, so as to confirm this account. But as Ansel Jenks, chief editor of the prestigious scholarly journal *Comics and Comedics*, would have it, "One need only look at the tape to see jealousy manifesting itself in the barbs and burlesques aimed all night at Douglas Myles." His was the name most mentioned that night, a glossy affair, the proceeds of which were to go, after expenses, entirely to war orphans in southeastern Europe. (The actual amount that made it across the Atlantic seemed a dubious number, causing a few comics, including Myles, to donate their already reduced appearance fees. But when have comics, since the days of Morris Gold and his "Dimes for the Displaced" campaign, not been the first of our entertainers to give, and by example lead the public?) Along with Rhino Stamps and Blum, the only name performer absent was Mandingo, himself touring Europe and donating portions of his receipts. But of those who entered that stage, whether Carlo Tarantella or Mr. Motormouth, Mindy Deskins or Jennifer Gean, Oz Paradise—conspicuously introduced that night as "King" Oz—all made concerted efforts to include in their routines some reference to Myles. Deskins, a pixieish blond who used her physical appearance as a perfect foil for her curse-riddled speech, was the first to perform, and after ten of her scheduled fifteen minutes, she slyly said, "Saw Douglas Myles backstage." She paused, as cheers emerged from the formally-clad crowd. "And I told him if he wants to 'do' me, he'd better buy me a fucking drink before and a goddam pack of cigarettes after!" Lamar Jackson followed, and though he and Myles at this time were no more than peers, out of gratitude for not mimicking him when they performed together, Jackson made no mention of him. "Though," he later said, "I could have if I wanted. At least ten comics asked if I was going to say anything about him. I told Mr. Motormouth, no, and he said, 'Do you need a capper?'" But, as alluded to earlier, Jackson was in a decided minority that night (other than being, along with Myles and Gonzalez, the only comics of color). After Deskins, some flouted his talent. Gonzalez did a passable imitation of him as a robot, with stiff head and arm movements, uttering in a mechanical voice, "Processing information. Processing information. Click, spring, boing! Vocal match achieved."

Others tried for audience sympathy. "Which would you rather hear," Tarantella boomed, "Myles's version or Carlo, the quello vero?" While Cousin Ezra drawled, "Back home my pappy always said imitations is the sincerest form of flattery. Don't y'all think so, too?" Perhaps the best line came, however, from the relative newcomer, Jennifer Gean, who'd been perfecting her postfeminist persona only a few years longer than Myles's career: "That's the good thing about having Myles go last. If you all don't get the jokes I say, he'll be more than happy to repeat them for you."

To some, this might seem the same complaint as David Blum's, but no one, especially Myles, had ever countered it to make it disappear. And if Gean's remark was a jab, in Oz Paradise's hands, this complaint became a weapon. Witnesses claim Paradise was angry that night, primarily for not being assigned the final slot, as Blum had always gotten at benefit shows when he was Comic of the Year. Instead, he had again his longtime penultimate position. "Never mind," wrote Owen Delaney in *The Jester*, "that he and Douglas Myles had equal billing and thirty minutes apiece. Never mind that he should have thanked the man for not raising a stink about the rigged Comics' Guild vote. Oz had to show who's king, and he wound up in the same place as Blum: messing with the wrong guy." It is of interest to note Paradise devoted his first fifteen minutes to his signature routine about airplane food and economy motels, yet he only seemed to gain his voice when he finished with that and turned on Myles. The audience did laugh, as they had with all the Myles-related calumny, but for a while, the professionals thought Myles should decline to appear, as Paradise all but scorched the stage with his rhetoric. In his writing, Myles ascribes to Paradise a Blum-like quality, where nothing from his mouth seemed anything more than a joke, yet on this night, the tall, bald, bearded comic dressed in black believed in what he said—or seemed to—with the fervor of an evangelical preacher. "I hope he'll do the 'History Lesson' tonight,"

Paradise said. "I know no one's tired of that." He closed his eyes and mimicked snoring. "I mean, come on, I keep a copy next to my bed. Works better than a tranquilizer and I don't need a prescription." Another five minutes of this passed, with laughter issuing, as Jackson said, "like steam from a pressure cooker." Paradise worked that vein until it was empty, then turned in a slightly new direction. "I mean, I kid. We all love the guy. But it must be nice to sit back on your ass and just wait for the rest of us to come up with new material. Then boom, turn on that tape player of a voice and you've got a brand new show, new record, comic of the . . . " He paused, fished about beneath his shirt. "Oh yeah," he said, brandishing the medallion he'd won and purportedly hadn't removed since. "You've got to earn that one!" Laughter shifted to applause and many patrons stood. Most comics say Paradise should have stopped there, but he continued his verbal screed: "I am and always will be the top dog. Just remember that when you hear my lovely voice coming out of the wrong head." Here he slammed the microphone to the stage—a bit stolen from Blum, who, in turn, had pilfered it from "Streetfighter" Archibald—and, arms raised above his glistening bald head like a champion prizefighter, he stalked into a jubilantly positive reception from his peers backstage.

The next morning, in the *Times*, Hector Cruz would write: "It was as transparent an effort as the *H.H. McCormick Show*. For no valid reason other than fear and jealousy, people ganged up on an unsuspecting Myles. Had I not seen his response to Blum two years ago, I might have felt sorry for him last night. But since I had, I was waiting to see what he'd have to say to 'King' Oz and his court." Naturally, many at home and in the audience assumed he would mimic Paradise, but Oz had done a wise thing in leaving the stage, assuring no exchanges between him and Myles. This, to the say the least, added to the anticipation. Too, there remained the question of whether Myles had heard any of Paradise's routine, or, for that matter, any of the ridicule aimed at him. When asked this by reporters the next afternoon, he first feigned he couldn't hear the question, then, when the persistent fellows couldn't be avoided, Myles remarked he hadn't heard anything, for he was meditating, as he did before every performance. A curious statement, as it's fairly antithetical to his discussion of pre-show gimmicks and rituals. He not once mentions meditation in his manuscript. From Lamar Jackson, we know that when they two performed, Myles would arrive in time to hear Jackson's act, but when alone or with another comic, he never appeared backstage until moments before his act commenced. On the night of the benefit, though, he was, as were all the comics, brought in by the producers early to pose for group and individual photos, videotape appeals to be shown during rebroadcasts and sign autographs which would be auctioned off. So it is certain he would have been backstage. But a recent reading of the manuscript has revealed an insight for this occasion, even though it doesn't refer directly to this benefit. (About this benefit show, he only writes: "At last you got to wear a tux.") A sentence, long overlooked as an illegible marginal scrawl—written in cursive instead of Myles's customary block print—was noted by a student of Greene's, Patricia Dunhill, who compared the letters to his signature and some other samples of his cursive and discerned the following: "Early on, you practiced being unseen." No one is sure what this refers to; the page on which it appears describes his first years in elementary school. But it's a provocative glimpse into the man, and, as Greene would have it, "Showing up out of nowhere certainly seems for him an appropriate act." And, on the night of the benefit, this could explain why no one, after the preliminaries of photos and such, could recall his presence. When they did see him, during the photo session, many asked what routine he'd perform, as he only had thirty minutes instead of the two- to two-and-a-half-hours he normally required. Jackson insists that to each person who asked, including himself, Myles replied, "A brief version of the 'History Lesson.'" And just before his name was called by the onstage announcer, a stagehand, who repeated this story the next day, asked, "Are you gonna do the 'History Lesson?'" Myles simply nodded. Yet, while behind the microphone, he neither introduced himself nor began with, say, "The Prince of Putdown's" "cracked kazoo" of a voice. His first words were, "I was wondering if I might have a volunteer, please."

The crowd, just settled down into the aching stomachs and sides that accompany so much laughter, did not hear him at first, so he repeated himself. Then the mimic removed the microphone, and, in a radical departure from form, began roaming the stage, until a young man sprinted up the steps, waved at the crowd and after Myles's odd request, spoke his name, hometown, age and marital status. For a long, still moment, no one in the audience, backstage, or even the young man, Jeff Gibbons of Paterson, twenty-one, single—"and ready to mingle," he appended in a waggish voice—no one sensed what was on the mimic's mind. That is, until he spoke into the microphone, reproducing the young man's words and voice, including Jeff's own variation, with such precision that the shocked inhalation of breath from so many at once sounded like the workings of a colossal pair of lungs.

It was, of course, a revision of Hernandez's "Impromptu" that Myles performed that night, and in thirty minutes, some ten people—male, female, black, white, an Asian couple in their seventies—stepped on stage, answered his questions, then stepped back dumfounded as out of Myles's mouth their own voices sprang. Had the comics backstage been students of the comedic past (and perhaps had Myles included Hernandez more in the "History Lesson"), they might have accused him of either stealing another comic's act, or assert he, like Hernandez, knew each one of these so-called volunteers and had learned their voices the night before. But, as Lamar Jackson would recall, "Most of us were looking on and listening like kids at a magic show." The only comic who didn't stay around to watch was Oz Paradise, who fled the scene and would, in two years time, follow Blum into the dusty obscurity of the state fair stages.

The next morning, the entertainment sections and not a few of the front pages featured headlines and articles detailing Myles's return. "He's Back!" read the *National Herald Daily*. "Better than Ever," crowed his hometown's *Dispatch*. "Amazing," was the comment of many readers, as well as "Did you hear Douglas Myles last night?" Mindy Deskins would say, "I think a lot of people felt they were really hot last night, but we weren't even on the same stage as him." The coverage was, in fact, so focused on Myles that a few reporters scarcely mentioned the other performers, let alone the worthy, philanthropic aim of the organizers who'd produced the benefit. It was Myles's show, and no one could deny that.

Among the scholars of today, one finds a host of reactions to the "Impromptu." Szok, ever the aesthete, will not deny the value of the "Impromptu" (or its eventual revisions), but considers it, "formless, without any artistic principles." For once, he finds in agreement with him Greene, who complains, "As a sheer physical performance, similar to an athletic feat . . . Myles's 'Impromptu' defies explanation. Yet, in the end, to borrow a complaint of David Blum's, it isn't very funny." Still, Melissa Tangier, whose independence from academic institutions, some feel, assures from her a less schematic view, declares this was the true height of accomplishment for Myles. Though, as many have said, she has only the tape of the benefit show, along with reviews and interviews, upon which to draw her analysis, she states: "He turned away from celebrity voices and shared the spotlight with ordinary people, making them as important, if only for a minute, as all the other voices he could summon. Yes, it might not be as funny as the 'Contemporary Scene' or as well made as the 'History Lesson,' but if for nothing more than inclusion and breaking down barriers, the 'Impromptu' reveals Douglas Myles as more than a comic or mimic but as an entertainer bar none."

The subsequent tour—two years long, with three months in our neighbor to the north and a whirlwind five weeks in the U.K. and Continent—broke attendance records of all sorts, pushing Myles from the confines of theaters to athletic arenas and outdoor stadiums, as tens of thousands, in every city, wished for their moment on stage. Myles was more accessible too, and people who came up could, if they were quick, touch him. A few female admirers even stole kisses, the subject of many a newspaper photo. And it was during this tour that he made his only two televised interviews after the *McCormick Show*. At thirty minutes each, with "rather vapid"—charges Szok—national network personnel, neither supplies much revelation about his performances, past or present, but one, on Union Broadcasting's *People U Should Know*, contains a salient bit of information. Asked what he looked for when trying to mimic, he said, "Over time I've tried to isolate exactly what separates that voice from all others. And rather than exaggerating or parodying it—which means to make fun—I try to reproduce it, as I hear it. Whether it's a cop or a congresswoman, I want to speak in her words and her voice."

He would not, however, on either program, answer personal questions. He would not even say "No comment" or "Next question." Instead, he'd stare at the interviewer until he or she moved on, as if saving his voice only for matters he deemed relevant. As well, he resisted attempts to elicit criticism of his peers, despite what many consider more than sufficient reasons to strike back. On both programs, he claims his ethnicity, twice on *Hanging Out With*, International Television Syndicate's competition for *People U Should Know*. But for the most part, he spends his time promoting the current tour and claiming that everyone has a voice that should be heard, and "not just from my lips." While some argue this was more of a transparent attempt to sell tickets, others, Melissa Tangier especially, declare, all along, this was one of Myles's prime concerns: making citizens aware of their own voices, not just how they spoke, but what they said, as well. In the end, though, the entire sixty minutes of tape (he speaks for approximately thirty-five of them) represent the longest recording of his own voice, something that Ansel Jenks avows is as valuable to scholars as the manuscript. Having viewed the two tapes some fifty times, Jenks maintains, "Beneath every answer . . . one can hear a glimpse, excuse the cliché, of the man behind the voices." While no one would ignore Jenks's argument completely—he is editor of the most influential journal of Comedic Studies—no other scholars have spent as much time with the tapes, as most view them solely in the light of Myles trying to promote the "Impromptu."

At first, the show ran about two hours and a half, enabling at least thirty people per night to stand next to him, whereupon they saw how small he was; women, older matrons particularly, mentioned how he looked as though he needed a good meal. Typically, in three minutes, they answered his questions, of which there were now eight: name, age, occupation, faith, marital status, favorite food, hobbies, and anything else one wished to share. Many volunteers, undone by the excitement, were rendered mute. They whispered their answers, while others spoke as naturally as they would at home and appeared more comfortable on stage than the mimic himself. A smaller but infinitely more entertaining group was made up of those who seemed to forget where they were and whom they stood by, as they rambled on, answering the questions out of order between sentence after sentence of extraneous facts. Yet with each group, Myles never requested any one speak louder, chastened none for hogging the spotlight, nor asked for a summarized version of a vocal peregrination.

Always, with each, he needed the same amount of time—
at most, twenty seconds—to wet his lips with his tongue,
close his eyes, and coax out, in whatever volume, tone, or
pattern, the voice everyone had just heard. Amos Wilson,
a native Bostonian of seventy-five years, married since he
was twenty to his beloved Delta (from the Magnolia State,
herself), employed for fifty-two years as an auto mechanic,
who took seriously the tenets of the Holy Mother Roman
Catholic Church and loved, more than any other dish,
chitlins and hot sauce—believe it or not!—and enjoyed
nothing more (other than time with his beloved Delta) than
wetting hooks in the Charles, told reporters the day after his
time with Myles, "I think in earlier times, before our modern
century, the boy would have been stoned for witchcraft. My
hand on the Holy Book, my voice, word for word, came out
of his mouth."

By the time Myles had left the East, after fourteen of
fifteen shows, one of which was canceled by a fire marshal
due to overselling of seats (Myles promised to reschedule
it), the publicity had reached his next stretch, the Southeast,
and waiting for him there were more people than there
were seats in most auditoriums. Ever the businessman, he
requested an adjusted appearance fee—from four to five
thousand; but, ever the entertainer, he promised to add
another fifty minutes, giving now ten more people a chance
to stand on stage. This maneuver, however, would satisfy
still only a lucky forty, which sent the patrons into a variety
of attempts to be among that number. No more did Myles
have to call for volunteers, as the ticket holders began lining
up on the morning of the show, then camping out the nights
before, heedless of their actual seat, desperate to stand by the
stage for as many hours as necessary. In Atlanta, enterprising
black youths rented themselves out to hold a space in line. A
scam, it turned out, as many of the teens claimed they had
bought the ticket, forcing the legitimate ticket holders to call
upon the police. When Myles learned of the shenanigans,

he invited the boys—some twenty-five of them—to be his guests at his performance on the following night.

By the time he reached the Lone Star State, after some thirty shows in forty nights, the theaters and auditoriums were deemed too small to hold the performances, so, for the first time, a comic was scheduled for the sports arenas that held ten to twenty thousand. A call went up in the press for him to give a little more time, and when he began his tour through the Golden State, Myles was reproducing some fifty voices in three and a half hours, but still, as he said on *Hanging Out With*, "I'm still disappointing about 9,950 people a night." Melissa Tangier writes, "Imagine those people who knew they weren't going to be in the 'Impromptu.' They came just to hear him. Amazing."

No stranger to the media since the *H.H. McCormick Show*, now his became a name mentioned nightly, not just in comedy clubs, but on news broadcasts in every city. Each night news cameras recorded the long lines and reporters interviewed the ticket holders, the evidence of which supports Tangier's analysis. Most admitted they wanted to make it up on stage, and there were those who sought to promote their new washateria or beauty salon, those who wanted to inquire about Myles's own marital status and if he were interested in changing it, along with a few budding comics who wanted to express admiration or "spar" with him. (The reviews either display that none of note occurred or that Myles's abilities clamped shut the mouths of any jokesters.) But whether in the Far West, Deep South, Great Plains or Myles's own Middle West, the reporters asked, "What if you don't get up there?" And to a one, the fans responded favorably; perhaps the best reply came from a pregnant young woman in Denver, who would not hear her voice from his lips that night, yet earlier said, rubbing her distended stomach, "I'll be able to tell my kids about him."

Such unqualified successes, though, no matter the field, do not exist without some setbacks. And when Myles moved from the hockey arenas to the outdoor stadiums, allowing upwards of thirty thousand to attend (his record being 47, 500 in his hometown), a few cities saw the need for mounted policeman to disperse crowds or quell squabbles among those without tickets who hoped to stay, as they had in the days of Banks and O'Meara, and listen to what they could discern from the parking lots. Ms. Foster's paternity suit was followed by one from Viola Edwards, three months later. (A total of six would be filed during his life.) At the time they emerged, Owen Delaney boasted, "This proves how popular he is. Only athletes and politicians get hit with those!" Supermarket tabloids occasionally ran headlines attesting to his freakishness. (Anton Greene keeps framed in his office a cover from the *Insider*, which features Myles shaking hands with a three eyed, six handed, potbellied alien, its headline trumpeting: "Alien to Comic: Keep 'Em Laughing . . . And VULNERABLE!") And when he sojourned to our northern neighbor, a skeptical reporter, one Murray Pollock from Toronto—a city that always seems suspicious of our nation's ways—began devoting his entertainment column in the *Crescent* to Myles's "Impromptu," presuming that at least some of the audience members were not locals. Pollock pointed to Hernandez's own scandal, and, in one column that appeared the night before thirty-thousand of his countrymen paid to see "the fraud," Pollock had this to say: "Common sense, which has never been in great abundance among our 'friends' to the south, should tell us that no man can, unaided, accomplish such a feat. Moreover, the sheer numbers, so typical of a nation prone to excess, suggests Mr. Myles isn't content with recreating a few voices. He insists on bigger, bigger and bigger, which suggests that an estimated third to half of his 'volunteers' are actually people paid to appear." Pollock promised to reveal this masquerade at the next night's performance, and, as if to facilitate him, Myles, after impersonating fifteen happy and dazzled folk, called Pollock up to the stage. ("Politely," most witnesses stated.)

Afterward Pollock would not back down from his central assertions, saying they had not been disproved, and as a celebrity himself, his voice was available on many accessible tapes for study. "Common sense," he wrote, "is still on my side." Despite all these subsequent protests, the audience members (their numbers now swelling like book pages left in water, as the story assumes legendary properties) avow that Pollock stood firm as Myles began reproducing his voice, but he swayed when the mimic continued, then, after Myles quoted from his column, toppled to the stage.

Others of Pollock's ilk waited for a misstep, though none were quite as adamant or vocal, and not all were members of the press. Myles's peers were as anxious to hear of a report from Alberta or Prince Edward Island that someone—a Caribbean immigrant, a Hutterite, or a child raised by foxes—would possess a voice or manner of speaking that he could not duplicate. At the time, Lamar Jackson was touring with Gonzalez and "Cuddles" (recently beginning his brief stay on the national circuit; diabetes would prevent his staying there long), and he mentioned how every morning in the hotel lobby, he watched the comical-looking duo page through the newspapers, then look up at one another simultaneously, shaking their heads "like the owners of a stock that never matures."

When Myles crossed the Atlantic after two years and, as Greene estimates, approximately 500 shows, an average of fifty fans a night, equaling 22, 5000 voices, a few believed that this would be the end, that the man—who'd just turned twenty-five—who'd never left his landlocked and provincial home state until his first trip to Manhattan, would find in one of the nations where English wasn't spoken a syllable or sentence he couldn't capture. This sentiment grew even stronger and more hopeful when it was announced, after Myles departed the United Kingdom—where his three London performances outdrew cricket and football matches combined—that he would not be using an interpreter.

Another legend has it that one flight from Detroit to Paris had Blum, Paradise and Pollock among its passengers, but as of this writing, that cannot be confirmed. Had this trio attended the sellout show, though, they would have spent their money in vain, and they would have felt the same in Vienna and Stockholm, Rome and Athens and during the finale—two nights in Moscow, where before a crowd of fifty thousand, Myles read his questions (written phonetically on a card; of Russian he didn't understand a word), and some eighty Muscovites, including a set of triplets, a speaker of Urdu, and a renowned opera Diva, passed by and heard, as one fellow said in halting English, "Myself speaking to myself." (Rumors abound about Myles and the Diva. After he trilled the same notes as she in conclusion to her answers—at a glass-shattering pitch—she hugged him energetically to her bosom and did not let loose until she'd kissed him frankly on the mouth. But this again seems just so much talk, as in the Diva's own diary (translated by Sergei Tarwid, a colleague of Greene's at the Pratt-Falls), she wrote of that night: "Alas, amazing as he is, he seemed when he had no voice to hide behind like a son more than a lover." Nonetheless, one wonders, as did Greene and Tarwid: "What kind of vocal power their progeny might possess?")

Most expected him to take time off upon his return to these shores. After all, the five weeks in Europe should have spent him, considering the amount of travel and effect of learning, albeit phonetically, six languages in four weeks. Yet not only did he continue—there was the matter of eight rescheduled shows—he brought to the "Impromptu" another wrinkle that made Hernandez's version (scandal and all, it was still a great feat) appear like the most pedestrian of parlor tricks. For once, an insight regarding his act appears in the manuscript; however, it does not appear in the section corresponding to this time of his life. (About Europe, he writes: "You never believed you'd get there, and when you left, it still didn't seem you'd been."

About his return: "You probably should have gone home, but there were too many people who wanted you in their town.") The particular passage can be found shortly after his account of his "discovery" by his kindergarten teacher, a time, it should be remembered, when the only people privileged to hear him were his immediate family and his maternal relations. He writes: "You would find yourself watching people, wondering if you could guess how they spoke. More often than not, you heard them correctly before they said a word." To some, this sounds like braggadocio, but given the facts, who can deny its truth?

The first of the eight shows was in Providence, where, two years earlier, the fire marshal could not be convinced that the numbers of tickets sold, which outnumbered the actual seats, was reason enough to let the show go on. (A year later, under ambiguous circumstances, the fire marshal was fired; allegedly, the mayor had held front row tickets.) Now the show was scheduled to take place in a football stadium that could hold, in the stands and on the field, thirty-six thousand. All of the tickets were sold in less than an hour, with, as the clerks would claim, some sold to buyers from as far away as the Sunshine State. The members of this massive crowd—though not the largest he'd played before—were told in advance not to line up, either on the night before or the morning of the show; instead, with each ticket one was given a questionnaire on which he or she were to record eight replies and ultimately drop it off in boxes near the entrances. A greater element of chance would exist now, and most people interviewed by the press were happy with this change.

Of course, more changes were to come, notably, that when Myles appeared, still in a nondescript suit (though some present thought it looked European, or at least finer in the fit and cut), he was pushing a large wheel barrow—his first prop, Jenks is quick to point out—in which lay the many questionnaires. Before bidding welcome, he plunged his hands in and pulled out two fistfuls of paper, then set them in an empty fishbowl placed on a stool next to the microphone stand. Next he began pulling the slips of paper out of the fishbowl and calling out, in his own voice, the names upon them. This resulted in many cheers and hollers and whoops as patrons leapt from their seats on the field and in the stands then dashed toward the stage. After fifty names, he stopped, then asked the lucky fifty to form a line to his left. A diverse group they were: among the fifty were military men, grandparents, fishermen, blacks, two manicurists, a lovely Latina sadly paralyzed from the waist down. "He couldn't have tried to put together a more different set of people," wrote Owen Delaney. Myles went rather quickly through the first nine, asking them to repeat what they'd written, shaping his voice to theirs in what seemed to most a shorter amount of time than at previous performances. But when he reached in and called out for Priscilla Petty and the spindly, red haired woman rushed toward the microphone stand, Myles held up his hand, silencing her. Everyone, audience members and those remaining on stage, looked on curiously. All must have wondered, "How can he mimic her without hearing her voice?" Then, in a voice that sounded, as one front row denizen would share, "like an out of tune accordion," Myles said, "I'm from Newport. I'm twenty-six and engaged to a wonderful man, I work as a receptionist at an insurance company. Obviously Catholic. I adore fried clams, strips, not the sandy bellies, and I'm into jogging with my fiancé."

Applause did not follow, as no one knew how well Myles had mimicked her, if he'd mimicked her at all. Though he held the card before him, many in the front rows said it appeared he wasn't reading from it. Only when Priscilla Petty, in a voice that nervously wheezed in and out of high and low registers—quite like an out of tune accordion—said, "Omigod, he's exactly right," did any reaction take place. However, it was mainly laughter, as the nervous receptionist

overlooked the fact Myles knew all her revelations because
she'd written them down for him. As the laughter reached
her, she clamped both hands over her mouth, let slip a
hearty laugh, then voiced what was slowly dawning on all
in attendance: "Omigod, he sounds exactly like me."

A few more out of the remaining forty would go through
a similar routine, and whether it was Ralph Vasquez,
machinist, Gregg Hirsch, the poet from Cambridge, Tina
Feeney, who loved breakfast sausage any time of day, or
Ms. Althea Monroe, "three time loser at the game of love,"
they all, before, indeed, their lips parted, heard their voice
confess to these and other replies as definitively as if they'd
spoken themselves. The subsequent standing ovation went
on for five minutes, though it did not lure Myles back out,
and, while exiting, the audience's mood was complete, and
summed up the next morning in the *National Herald Daily*'s
front page headline: "Maybe the Tabloids Are Right?"

The Blum prediction returned to many minds, and an
interest in ascribing psychic powers to Myles was resurrected.
In some quarters, this meant praise, while in others, it meant
condemnation. Not a few ministers—especially those with
poor television ratings—used this performance as a sign of
wickedness in the land, although their sermons did little to
prevent the faithful from praying, when the "Impromptu"
came to town, that they'd be selected as one of Myles's chosen
few. Myles went about completing the remaining shows,
ignoring or overlooking the daily editorials and demands
he be given a thorough examination (or exorcism) in order
to see what went on in his miraculous throat and mind.
Yet nothing offstage shook him, nor did anything onstage,
including the motorcycle gang that interrupted his show in
Omaha's Municipal Field. That hirsute and greasy crew had
no malevolent designs; they simply wanted to let him try
them, which, after telling security he was okay, Myles did,
reproducing all twelve's "rattling and raucous" voices after
reading their names off the badges sewn on their leather

vests.

Looking back, over the distance of many years, it was probably best that he performed this version of the "Impromptu" as few times as he did. At the final show, in the still-standing Emerald Dome in Seattle, two hundred thousand arrived to buy tickets, leaving behind empty shops and offices and snarling vehicle traffic for hours. Today one hears doubts over whether or not actually Myles accomplished what is professed. Some maintain his mimicry wasn't truly that accurate or as pitch-perfect as those he executed after hearing the speaker, though those who were impersonated or in attendance—many of whom Tangier has interviewed—will quickly and enthusiastically counter that, saying, as Afis Kawanga of Chicago's Northside (by way of Ghana) did: "I know my own voice. And that is precisely what I heard from him." No evidence has been uncovered to support this next claim, but others believe that those selected—including the Omaha Chapter of the Devil's Spawn—were plants. As well, an article, "The Volunteering Nature of Volunteers," was written ten years later by El Jefe, a famous magician who also debunked paranormal activities. He takes a different tack, intimating that often people are so excited to be near a performer that they reveal much to him, and that perhaps during these moments, a sly Myles was able to muffle the microphone, or turn it off so none but he could hear the speaker. Still, El Jefe's article was published too late to change many minds. Nothing, from any source, could affect the admiration held for him in a considerable part of the civilized world. And to all this, did he say anything? Not publicly, of course, but Lamar Jackson swore that when he asked him, years after the last performance of the "Impromptu," what was the secret, Myles said, "I've always been a good guesser."

Then, at this stage of success, he removed himself from the scene again. This time, though, he was away for two full years, without any of the performances or promotions that attended his previous absence. No visits to the Laughter Lounge and only a pair of them to Chuckles, where he did no mimicry onstage or off-. No records, despite a number of offers. No books in the tradition of the joke collections authored by Lucky Chance and David Blum, no obviously ghostwritten autobiography such as "Streetfighter" Archibald's. No benefit shows, though his charitable contributions were many. No surprise TV appearances or studied endorsements of products. Today, scholars believe he was worn down after the number of performances and required the time away, but in his day, audiences clamored for some glimpse of his face, better yet, the sound of his altered voice. In adulation and fear he might not perform again, some tracked down his address. When called upon, he could be, it is reported, quite civil, inviting strangers inside—including those who pocketed forks and watches and neckties as mementos—and serving drinks while asking them questions. However, no plea could elicit from him an impersonation. Few personal questions, no matter how heartfelt, received an answer, save for when the fans asked, "What can we do to bring you back?" In his own voice, he'd reply, obliquely, "Give to those in need."

Some might conclude that his two years away marked a bad time for comics and comedy, yet history shows it was anything but. While Myles was not in view, his peers certainly were, and in the first year of his exile, revenue generated by ticket and record sales increased slightly from the phenomenal numbers of Myles's last year with the "Impromptu." The next year would see revenue level off, but at an average of forty dollars per week spent by the average household, no one should imagine any suffering professional comics. In fact, Greene insists that part of Myles's legacy was to advance professional comedy to a level where theater tours no longer represented the pinnacle of achievement: now, routinely, comics play in hockey and basketball arenas, and, when in package tours, baseball and football stadiums. While sport remains, even today, the entertainment most of our nation's citizens spend money on, these years of Myles's absence represent the time when comedy very nearly overtook it, and the two combined left other recreations to fight for the few dollars remaining.

In the context of Myles's legacy, though, a scouring of newspapers and magazines of that time reveals that among the comics there were few, if any, mimics. Unlike the days of O'Meara, Simpkins and Salvatore, no host of fellows toiled in the smoky taverns, waiting for their opportunity at the celebrity afforded their more famous peers. Ansel Jenks concludes, "No one could be influenced by him. He was so good he was intimidating." Szok writes, "Just as he'd been when he was starting out . . . he was the entire movement." Not that the other comics minded the absence of Myles-influenced competition. Lamar Jackson said, "We knew we were in his shadow when he was performing, but when he was off the stage, and no other mimics were there to take his place, a lot of us were like those guys who go out with their friends' girls when the friend's away at school. And you know what tends to happen in those situations."

Jackson himself is a perfect example: long-considered a second-tier comic, one who headlined at clubs and warmed up for luminaries in theaters, he'd given up his "black nerd" act and developed routines that maintained the veneer of observational comedy while interjecting a kind of satire found in the finest work of the social critics. As Myles's second year away began, Lamar Jackson was increasingly touted as "today's most influential comic," especially for his award-winning routine on stereotypes, "Eating Watermelon in Public." Soon "Speedy" Gonzalez would stun many by dropping his nickname and demanding the new billing of Jesus (conveniently forgetting his given name was Jason), while Mindy Deskins made a point of dropping all obscenities, stopped wearing make-up, and thrilled female audiences with her gender politics. Melissa Tangier writes, "The aim of these comics was still to get laughs, no doubt about it. Jackson and Gonzales, the new fellows like Curtis Steele, Jimmy Ng, Amos Drinkwater, as well as the female comics influenced by Mindy Deskins—Lupe Morales and Tracey Fine—they still told a lot of jokes, but they wanted you to think a little bit on the drive home." And this new direction, Szok asserts, could not be welcome to any of the older generation, many of whom either had, like Rhino Stamps, quit touring and opened a club, or still prowled the stages of lesser circuits, like Blum and Oz Paradise. Others tried to adapt, but Cousin Ezra, Carlo Tarantella and even the venerable Dena Cuomo and Mr. Motormouth were hinting that retirement was not far off for them.

This question remains, though: what, if any, impact did this development have on Myles? Inasmuch as one could say he'd been influenced by no one of his generation, it wouldn't seem likely that he'd be measuring the comedic winds to alter his performances. But he most certainly would have been aware of what was going on, in part through the postcards he received from Lamar Jackson, who also reminds us that Myles was an avid television viewer for most of his life. So he had to have seen the changes. It seems he would have liked to hear these new routines, having found truth lacking in the material of most. But as he makes no direct mention anywhere, just how much the new turn in professional comedy may have influenced him—especially with his subsequent "Family Hour"—is difficult to say.

What is known, though, is that as the ground shifted, many desired to see Myles return from what seemed more and more like a retirement than a rest. Sixteen months into his absence, editorials began to emerge, pondering if he'd hung up his microphone for good. A desire for certainty grew great among the press. Yet all interview requests were turned down. "Politely," most say, revisiting a word one finds over and over in reference to his demeanor. More fans were knocking on his door at odd hours, which eventually produced a security checkpoint at the opening of his dead end street, where a team of security guards (their salaries paid by Myles) made sure, in deference to his neighbors, that no one entered between the hours of nine a.m. and nine p.m.

In print and aloud, over the TV and over dinner, reporters and citizens quested vainly for what might bring him back. Money wasn't an issue, as any could tell how humbly he lived, and estimates of how much he'd earned on the "Impromptu" tour reached the millions. Fans held out hope that a neophyte comic might err by insulting him, necessitating a timely response. And this, to some degree, occurred on an episode of the *H.H. McCormick Show* (its ratings slipping and its host looking worn and gray), when Curtis Steele, a young black comic, was asked about the great black comics of the past. Steele quickly mentioned Mandingo, Jackson, of course, and even the social critic Martin Love, whom he'd only heard on recordings. Wearily, McCormick said, "But what of Douglas Myles?" Steele said, "I never really saw him as black." While it seems most felt about Myles as Steele did—that his race was unnoticeable or irrelevant—the comedy audience manufactured some indignation while it waited for their hero's response. None came. Not in a week or a month. Another month passed and though Lamar Jackson publicly and privately chastised his protégé for the blunder, still no reply came from Myles. A reporter called to inquire after his health, to which he replied he was fine. The reporter then said, "While I have you on the line, did you happen to hear what Curtis Steele said about you?" To which, Myles lied, "I don't really watch much TV. Thanks." Then he hung up.

At this point, the press exhibited a turn toward mourning, as editorialists worried that Myles's career had quietly ended. What would happen in a world without his performances, they asked. A particularly lugubrious title read, "Will We Laugh Again?" But this moribund period did not last very long: soon the focus became of gratitude, and writers reflected on the three tours, the one record, the countless joy the man had given. Owen Delaney, in a Jester issue devoted entirely to Myles, summed up the mood best: "No one ever said the party would last forever. And when it seems things are winding down and all the guests are nearing the door, it's time to take a moment and make sure the host knows our appreciation. Now, I'm not saying this is it for Myles, but if it is, he shouldn't see long faces. We should be clapping as loudly as we did when he stepped on stage."

At his house, which visitors, even today, often remark upon as being as nondescript as one of his suits, the visits increased, but with order and respect to the man rather than spontaneous knocks and demands he impersonate a girlfriend at six in the morning. They left huge cards at the security checkpoint, signed by every member of a Comedic Studies seminar or fan clubs from Duluth and Poughkeepsie (none were official, as, unlike most of his peers, he'd never established one of these profitable enterprises). A high school chorus sang "Happy Birthday" outside his door, leaving with the guards roses by the dozens. One legend has it that, on a cool October night—two weeks before Myles announced his return—Blum and Stamps, by now a pair of humbled men, nearing eligibility for Comic Guild pensions, stopped by to apologize, and were received by Myles, staying with him until the small hours of the morning. Unverifiable and likely untrue—Ansel Jenks alleges an unrepentant Blum, on his deathbed, whispered, "I'm still funnier than that Mynah bird"—but this tale, and a host of others, featuring Oz Paradise, Carlo Tarantella, and all the other comics whom Myles surpassed, reveals the mindset of the fans at the time. They seemed both somber and reverential, as if it were the twenty-seven-year-old Myles on his last legs in life.

While no one should suggest this outpouring was all for naught, what is clear is that it was premature. For soon, amidst all the professions of respect and endearment, Myles was planning his newest, and last, routine, the "Family Hour." A very comic image it is: fans outside his windows singing or leaving behind tokens to the guards (who gathered so many stuffed animals that the local Child Welfare office lacked no toys to give their wards for years); meanwhile, inside, in climate controlled privacy (Jackson maintains Myles liked it frosty), their idol perfects his newest performance.

When exactly he knew he would perform the "Family Hour" is not known, though the manuscript contains this general reference: "You never sat down wondering what to do next. Before a tour started to wind up, a new set of voices would invade, and you'd be fighting to finish off one tour without changing your act." Thus, one might point to the last months of the "Impromptu," which certainly challenged him physically but may not have been as satisfying as his "Master's Act," the "Contemporary Scene" and the "History Lesson." Having performed it so long, even with his tinkering and, some say, perfection, he might have been ready for something new even earlier. With either speculation, though, what is one to make of the time between his last "Impromptu" and the opening night of the "Family Hour?" Myles himself writes: "You didn't intend so much time off. You wanted to fall asleep in your own bed for a few nights. When you woke up, though, it seemed a year had passed by." Parenthetically, and ruefully, he appends: "(Sometimes, you wished you hadn't waked up at all.)"

The record shows that two years and two months after his last "Impromptu," he contacted, with the request for limited publicity, the programming director at the Palace Theater in his hometown, a venue that had featured all the mimics of the past—one will remember, Rhino Stamps had performed there on that fateful night—yet, in his dizzying ascent, Myles had never trod its boards. The programming

director, Sheryl Cline, would say, after he allowed her to
publicize the performance, that when an assistant told her
Douglas Myles was on the line she was prepared to "tell
the crackpot to go to hell and hang up." But Ms. Cline
would speak to him and subsequently scratch a chamber
orchestra from those two nights he requested (ticket sales
had been sluggish besides) and announce to her staff a
need for secrecy, then allow them a five-minute period of
unabashed giddiness. In the time of Myles's exile, the Palace
had not seen a full house, and, seeing the comics that had
once filled it now moving on to sports arenas, the owners
were grumbling of a sale to a cinema corporation from the
Keystone State. An appearance by Myles, Ms. Cline believed,
would renovate the old building better than any cans of
finish or team of carpenters. Yet it should be noted that she
and her five person staff—though "busting at the seams to
tell people"—kept their secret admirably, as no one outside
knew of the performance until a week in advance, when
Myles approved and paid for a simple ad to be published
on the back page of the *Dispatch*'s front section.

"FAMILY HOUR," it read. "A new performance by
Douglas Myles. November 3 and 4 at the Palace." No
photos or details of what material the show might contain,
yet, by this time, nothing superfluous was needed to attract
hordes. Suffice it to say, this was a moment many were
anticipating. Delaney, in his *Memoirs of a Laugh-o-holic*,
speaks of tortured souls, himself included, who came across
enigmatic advertisements and arrived at obscure venues,
certain the performer was Myles under a pseudonym,
only to find no one doing anything like mimicry on stage.
After the ad appeared, the *Dispatch* and the Palace's phone
operators received thousands of calls from frantic fans
seeking confirmation of what sounded more dream than
reality. The four thousand available tickets sold in twenty-
six minutes, despite such Myles-initiated contrivances of
two seat maximums; the lines stretching around the theater

held up traffic, requiring police assistance to return things to normal. Immediately, on the streets, scalpers charged five hundred a ticket, increasing their rates to a thousand by the first scheduled night of the performance. A non-profit organization—Race Unity—auctioned off a pair of front row seats donated by Myles and received a winning bid of seven grand from an anonymous bidder (variously rumored to be the Russian opera Diva, Oz Paradise, and an organized crime kingpin). Network and national press representatives arrived en masse, booking entire floors of hotels and badgering Ms Cline for press passes, which she was instructed to give only to local reporters. Still, no one left. They adapted, or, in a few cases, made auspicious promises in trade for passes. Though Myles had hoped to have reviewers from the local weeklies for minority readers, most, if not all, gave away their passes, as the amount of money many national writers were willing to part with, in one case, surpassed the annual advertising budget of the *Messenger*. As well, Tangier asserts: "a lot of local journalists believed they were exchanging their press passes for a ticket to national publications and network shows."

The week sped by. In the Buckeye State, the weather cooled, it being November, Myles's least favorite time of year: "You wished it would hurry up. Get to the snow and ice of January so Spring might come sooner." Security around his house and neighborhood increased. In twelve-hour shifts, two six-man teams patrolled the checkpoint and the surrounding streets to maintain a perimeter. They were promised lucrative bonuses for absolute silence, prompting the rumor that all twelve were mutes. With reporters and fans alike trying to find some scrap that indicated what or—better yet—whom he'd be doing, they thronged the streets and tried to gain entry through backyards. When they knocked on the doors of his eight neighbors, they found the houses empty, all the inhabitants vacationing in the Caribbean or Old Mexico, their travel paid for by Myles.

The phone must have been ringing twenty-four hours a day at his house, especially when the hours started to near the time of his performance. Yet no one heard his voice, even Owen Delaney and Hector Cruz, who both believed — wrongly, it turned out — with their national prominence and past support of Myles, that they'd at least get a preliminary summary of the act. The hours ticked away, the temperatures dropped, and, at last, on November third, the Palace lit up as it hadn't since the early days of the observational comics, and the doors opened.

One wishes for a film or at least an audio recording of the "Family Hour," yet there are not even still photos of the performances, and the reviews, written by people who were, at best, bewildered, at worst, disappointed, don't begin to detail all that Myles did on that first night and the second, where he stopped forty minutes in and exited the stage. ("Not in a hurry," writes Hector Cruz, who paid a scalper fifteen hundred for two nights, "but like someone trying to follow a whisper.") Given the build up and anticipation that Myles tried to limit but could not, one wonders what exactly he could have done to please the crowds, having to compete against his past performances, as well as the imagined ones with which ticket holders had arrived at the Palace. Szok attributes the failure of the "Family Hour" to the success of the "Impromptu": "By allowing the fans to share the stage ... he could never afterward ask them to sit tight and just listen." Indeed, restlessness was described by most reviewers, as was the counterfeit laughter accompanying the first thirty minutes. However, the Saturday papers do not display any outright condemnation, as all of the writers preceded with caution and hesitance. Many asserted uncertainty and a dearth of clearly comic routines, and they qualified their reviews with such statements as the following, that appeared in the *Dispatch*: "What Douglas Myles hopes to accomplish with the 'Family Hour,' at present, is unclear. Then again, we should remember his previous masterpieces, and how they weren't as obvious as punch lines in their first performances." This was not authored by Clayton Adams III, of course; D. Graham LaSalle wrote it, one of his last pieces before beginning a nationally syndicated column. (One wonders if LaSalle exchanged his press pass on either night.) And this new crop of critics, Tangier states, "were not those who viewed Simpkins, Hernandez, or even the social critics. These were the children who'd been weaned on David Blum and Mr. Motormouth." In other words, as Tangier goes on to say, Myles now faced "an audience for whom subtlety is a whispered obscenity."

That said, however, the Sunday reviews achieved the widest audience and very well may have brought to an end the "Family Hour," unless one considers Myles was ending it when he walked off stage. These, in the words of Owen Delaney, "were brutal." Hector Cruz, who, along with Delaney, was old enough to remember the social critics, offered some measured praise, claiming that clearly this was a preliminary performance, and that, "once Mr. Myles clears the bugs out—as we suspect he will—there is no doubt this will be a performance that dazzles." His, though, is the only such voice. The rest appear, even to today's reader, as venomous as snakes and twice as deadly. "We waited all that time for this?" reads one lead. "The stage rust was covered with more rust," reads another. Some pointed to how quietly the mimic spoke, as if uncertain, and how no one knew the subjects of his mimicry. Others pointed out that it went too fast, few noting that he had ended prematurely. All seemed to battle for the most cutting of phrases, as if forgetting how much praise he had earned in the past. In the end, the one most dismissive and ultimately reflective of all who attended, was this, from Rex Humphrey, his former champion, now writing for a Cleveland paper: "Myles sucked."

But what of the actual performance of the "Family Hour?" Using the reviews, Myles's own manuscript, statements allegedly made to Lamar Jackson and the accounts of others in attendance, a vague reconstruction can be attempted, but as for Myles's intentions, some guesswork must be done. It is known that when the curtains parted, one saw a television set, surrounded by two chairs, a stool and a long couch— "suitable for four or five people to sit comfortably," Sheryl Cline mentions. The TV was outmoded and large, topped with rabbit ear aerials, while playing on its screen, silently, was a black and white loop of Simpkins, O'Meara, Banks, and Salvatore. Szok suspects this tape is an homage not simply to the masters who preceded him, but a signal to the careful viewer of Myles's own avant-garde roots. And given the customary public response to anything cutting edge— absolute rejection—one could easily link the "Family Hour" to his early days at the Hub. What most believe, though, is that the scene is a domestic one, the furniture and TV of a vintage that suggests his own youth.

After a moment or two, he emerged from the wings. He acknowledged the crowd with a nod, the faraway look in his eyes even more distant, especially on Saturday night. His dress was typical: brown suit on Friday, blue on Saturday. He looked thin, but not sickly, and his hair was trimmed to its usual stubbly length. Aside from the domestic scene behind him—his fullest use of props, Ansel Jenks reminds—the only difference about his appearance was the small microphone clipped to his lapel, an addition which struck many reviewers as curious: he'd always used a hand held before. Along with the TV and the furniture, the microphone suggested changes, and all waited breathless to see the form following the function.

At this point, opinions widely diverge. He did, no matter whom one reads, sit down both nights, on one of the chairs, which angled him away from the audience. What he said is now lost, in whose voice, one can only surmise, but the pattern was set: for the next hour and a half, Myles moved from chair to chair, chair to stool, stool to couch, couch to other cushions, then to the floor and back. Through the mic, what he said was always clear, but a common complaint, voiced after the show and reported in reviews, was "he never looked at us." It should be said that the mimic never looked at anyone during his performances. Even those fortunate enough to stand beside him during the "Impromptu" struggled to lock their eyes on his, often to see his shut lids. Still, on these two occasions, the lack of eye contact suggested more of a lack of confidence on Myles's part, as if, Sheryl Cline said, "He wasn't sure he wanted to share with the crowd." To all this, though, Cruz remarks that during the last fifteen minutes of Friday's "Family Hour," Myles stood from the floor and faced the Palace audience, which should have satisfied the desire for a better, more intimate connection, but what had plagued the show and "caused a lot of people to turn whispering to their neighbors," according to Cruz, was that no one knew to whom any of these voices belonged. In a way, he'd circled back to his stage origins, only this time there was no one in the crowd to affirm to the rest that every voice he reproduced was dead-on and that he was, without question, a genius.

After Friday's long impression facing the audience, Myles turned around and turned off the television. The curtains fell then, but on Saturday he never got past the couch. At first he hesitated, almost seated himself, then walked off. Some state they heard him curse—venturing a guess at every blue word ever coined—but given his sense of decorum this seems highly unlikely, though, as Tangier clarifies, "To be certain of anything from these performances is impossible, as a very different Douglas Myles was on that stage."

What were the impressions, one wonders. In the manuscript, Myles writes, "The voices always indicated the direction you went," which almost suggests a control over him not unlike that which his kindergarten teacher had earlier feared. Maddeningly, though, he does not specify which voices, at this time, were leading him, and to where they were headed. Among the contemporary reviewers, there were guesses that he was doing the voices of "Impromptu" volunteers or that he was doing a variation of the "History Lesson" but selecting comics too obscure to recall. Cruz, particularly adept, identified ten different voices, all of which corresponded with a place on the stage. As well, he discerned four female voices and six male, though, in the end, all he could conclude was, "What this group of people—a family of some kind—are up to, only Douglas Myles knows."

Today, it seems odd that no one—and this is the case with all thirty-nine reviewers who managed their way in—guessed that the family was his own. Perhaps it was because he seemed, at times, to have emerged fully formed, that people never thought of him as having a family or for that matter cared, as long as he astonished with his prowess. Perhaps the advantage of distance has today made this suggestion of the voices being those of his family more clear—that and the manuscript, though few have considered that document a compendium of direct clues. Nonetheless, one still hears advanced some baroque possibilities, far stranger than the guesses of the contemporary reviewers. Prahtva Griggs, a student of Szok, has written in *Comics and Comedics* that "the voices absolutely don't matter. I wouldn't be surprised to learn that they weren't even the same both nights, as the intent seems sabotage: Myles wanted to quit performing and this was a way to bring about that end." Audacious, yes (then again, all Szok's students are) but it reduces the mystery in too convenient a manner. Given the title, the set, the unfamiliarity experienced by the audience, it seems the voices had for the mimic a more private luster and indicate a direction—celebrities to real people to his own, since departed relations—that is as curious as the man himself. Was it even, in his own mind, a comic endeavor? This last point is raised by Greene, who posits that Myles's intentions might not have even been humorous. He points to the contemporary reviewers, and how no one knew what to laugh at, because Myles never paused, allowing the space for reaction. "Quite frankly," Greene insists, "one might see Myles as author, director and actor of a play. Not a one-man show, but one man as the entire cast. A fairly radical departure for the comic and dramatic conventions of the day." More enticing, however, is one of Jackson's recollections, for though he was touring at the time and unable to attend either night of the "Family Hour," he did tell Owen Delaney that he once overheard Myles mumbling, "warm brass of Gran," over and over and this ten years before the discovery of the manuscript. Why, though, with all his apparent desires for privacy, would Myles reveal so much personal material in a performance? Did he long for those simpler days when he was still surrounded by family? Was the last impression of the act, where he faced the audience, a version of his younger self? Did he believe an audience, which he knew would be expecting the excesses of the "Impromptu," would accept this?

In the end, as Jenks reminds, one thing and one thing alone is certain about the "Family Hour": "No one liked it. Douglas Myles didn't do it on stage a complete two times. And he never performed it again."

Throughout the history of Comedic Studies, a general tension has existed over which "side" needs most attention, as witnessed in the title of Jenks's esteemed journal, the comic or the comedics. In particular, much debate consists over whether to continue the study of a comic until his or her death or to consider the material only. Early on, biographers like L. P. Chance ruled the day, because her subjects never quit performing. Even when the one-liner royalty and vernacular storytellers were in their eighties, they played the state- and, worse, the county-fair circuits, telling the jokes they'd told in their twenties, often not stopping until they, like Roth, Gold, and Daffy Dan Dukes, met their mortal end on stage. Chance's disciples, Greene, Szok, Jenks, and Tangier favor performance analysis, with some biography, along with the rigorous consideration of cultural influences. (Not a few of their students—the third generation—avow that the comic is but a vehicle of the comedics, and requires little, if any, attention.) But Myles resists categorization always, and unlike those before him and his peers, he surprised all then and surprises today, for he did not, as some predicted, return to the "Impromptu" and barnstorm smaller venues, where he might have crossed paths with Blum or Paradise. Nor did he open a club of his own, like Rhino Stamps, or, like Mr. Motormouth and Dena Cuomo, who'd married around the time of the "Family Hour" after years of a secret courtship and would, on occasion, at their club, Sir Laff-a-lot's, be coaxed on stage by the audience. Myles simply stopped. Once a few months passed after the Palace debacle, a few writers suggested that, as in the previous absences, no one would see or hear from Myles for a considerable amount of time. Some even predicted he'd go into hiding forever, and only at his funeral would he be visible again. As if in defiance of this foreboding note, he commenced what some call the second phase of his public life, as a philanthropist. Others contend he had been doing charitable works all along, and that now he was only becoming more public while encouraging others to follow his lead. Among the charities and foundations he represented, most sought to remedy inequities created by race, class and gender, factors, as he wrote in a letter for the League of Cities Charity, "many would rather convince themselves don't exist instead of trying to mend." In this way he was visible for about five years, visiting around the country, arriving at squalid tenements and tarpaper shacks with food, clean clothing and checks. He wrote letters appealing to the munificence of all, employing a prose style far more elaborate than that of his manuscript. One, still extant, reads, in part, "As a black man, and former entertainer, I have encountered successes beyond measure. Yet I assure you that mine and a few others' blessings are not shared by all. I have a reason and the wherewithal to give. I urge you, *in my own voice*, to look within and around, to see if there are not conditions needing your aid [emphasis added]." Tangier likes to point out that though he obviously no longer viewed himself as an entertainer, "no one believed he was completely finished." Lamar Jackson, who by this time had edged out his competitors to become the first black to win Comic of the Year award from the Guild, didn't believe Myles was done. He speaks of a visit to Myles's house, where, while serving dinner (Myles rarely dined out; a habit, he writes, stemming from his childhood: he and his parents never ate at restaurants), he asked Jackson about their peers—his former, Jackson's current—then with a deadpan expression spoke of each with an effortless duplication of their voice. "He'd been practicing," Jackson says. "I was pretty sure of that."

Rumors floated around, suggesting a new record in the works, book deals, a resurrection of the "Contemporary Scene," adding on the new voices of Jimmy Ng, Curtis Steele, Lupe Morales, and others. On occasion, tabloid headlines would affirm he weighed three hundred or ninety pounds, that he never cut his hair or shaved it twice a day or that he was responsible for the disappearance of runaways (intimating he quaffed virginal blood to strengthen his vocal powers). With his phone number still listed in the white pages, any one could call and discover that none of the rumors were true, but, as before, every entreaty to perform was politely rejected. If a benefit show was in development, he'd send a large check—one, to Race Unity, for one point five million— and write a letter of support to be duplicated, but nothing lured him back. To those who saw him during this period—his neighbors, Jackson—he appeared happy, a man with certainty and purpose in his life, who never betrayed a sign of regret or a desire to return. The charities he sponsored collected millions, and in many cities and depressed rural areas, one still finds youth centers he helped to build, and children who attended universities on scholarships bearing his name. Myles writes, "You had to become a name first. Else no one would listen."

Somewhere around this time—he'd just turned thirty-two, over ten years had passed since the *H.H. McCormick Show*—he may have begun writing. Perhaps he had in mind a book, perhaps he was bored. But a distinct change came over him, and about this period of life, he writes, "You think there's no place to go anymore." The ambiguity of "place" strikes many scholars, for one certainly wonders if Myles felt he'd reached a nadir or if he'd simply grown tired of being recognized at supermarkets and being asked to reproduce the voices of great-uncles named Clyde. Lamar Jackson still visited Myles once a year, when he came to town to perform. He was then earning ten thousand a show ("All thanks to Myles's raising the bar," he'd say) and performing at football stadiums, but the mimic would never attend, not even to view from backstage. During one visit, Jackson heard on the radio some devastating news. He was crying as the cab passed the unoccupied security post near Myles's street, and crying still when he knocked on the door. "Mandingo just died," he told Myles, who for a brief moment said nothing. Later, Jackson would describe the visit, saying, "He seemed stunned, as I was at first. So I reached out for him, and my hand touched his shoulder, but he jumped back. He shook his head. 'Another one gone," he said. 'Another one to remember. I can hardly keep them straight anymore.' I asked what he meant, which was a question I asked him a lot. And, as always, he shook his head, and said, 'Nothing.'"

In tandem with the ambiguity of what he meant by "no place to go," this moment presents Myles in a light that brings back a parenthetical aside from the manuscript, where he asserts the early mimics did not know "the greatest risk" of their art. As the only other among the greats who died long after his career ended is O'Meara, one might agree with Myles, sensing that somehow the ability to mimic could cause some mental damage, making the artists feel they must continue to record the voices of the people they knew. Clearly, other comics kept performing, and their material, though unchanged from their heydays, did not seem to affect the men offstage. Jenks insists that Blum was as mentally sharp in his final years as he was at the height of his powers. L.P. Chance's biographies of Uncle Ike and "Streetfighter" Archibald show them to be perfectly lucid until their deaths, and both of them lived into their eighties. Had Myles reached out to the world more, the onset of any aberrant behavior might have been diagnosed and perhaps even stopped, but that still wouldn't have prepared anyone for the event that brought his name back into the news, an event that, according to Tangier, "Should break your heart if you have one."

All along, as stated, the tabloids reported on Myles, yet he wasn't at all singled out. Charges of his degeneracy and hermithood were similar to charges they'd attached to other celebrities who'd willingly or unwillingly left the public arena, and hardly treated as serious by the masses. But when Myles's name appeared first in the front section of his hometown's *Dispatch*, the news seemed nothing to laugh at or ignore. In his neighborhood, no one considered him a celebrity. It had been ten years since the "Family Hour," and now he house sat for neighbors on vacation, raked leaves, doled out candy at Halloween, and sent Xmas cards to all. No one at the grocery store remarked on his presence during his twice-weekly visits, though never did he have to show an ID when he wrote a check. One morning, however, a group of three white men, cousins of one of Myles's neighbors, visiting from the Hoosier State, sighted him, and, as their spokesman later told reporters, "dropped our cookies and ran over to meet him." It had been some time since the mimic was subject to such a response, and the trio was not a group of young men: they were all in their late twenties and craving to "talk to a real celebrity." This meant handshakes and autographs and a slap to Myles's back that, according to other witnesses, "almost knocked him to the ground." From here, let the reporter's account tell the rest:

> *Mr. Myles made an attempt to depart, but the three men wanted to hear him do an imitation. Mr. Powell said, "We'd heard he could do those ones where he didn't even have to hear you talk. And my brother Ed hadn't said anything yet. He was in awe, right? So we wanted to see could he do Ed."*
>
> *Mr. Myles again attempted to leave. Witnesses say the young men surrounded him and grew very loud. "I heard a threat," said Ms. Janis Clemons, of Whitehall. At last, Mr. Myles spoke, in what would later be learned was an impersonation of an old nemesis of his, "King" David Blum, a master of insults. Mr. Myles was quoted as saying, in Blum's voice, "They call me the king, because when you mess with me, you get crowned."*
>
> *That he resorted to Blum's catch phrase, some think, reveals that the young men, though lacking malicious intent, must have presented to Myles a fearsome front. One might speculate as well that there may have been similar conflicts in his youth, resulting from his being the only child of mixed race. He does not write of them in the manuscript directly, but for what else would he "practice being unseen" but to avoid conflict? However, what happens next shows things quickly growing worse:*
>
> *Witnesses state that the cousins now demanded Mr. Myles comply with their request, though the men deny this.*

*They also deny that one of them shoved Mr. Myles. At this
point, all eyewitnesses agree Mr. Myles began to insult the
cousins in a high-pitched voice, then continued in a deeper
voice. He broke away from them and shouted in another
voice, "Pappy, I never knowed these city folk could be so
durn mean."*

*As a mimic, the Buckeye state native set attendance
records, and, of late, has done much charitable work, though
little has been heard from him in the past several years.*

"I don't know which is worse," Tangier said during a
recent roundtable on Myles's career held at the Pratt-Falls.
"The incident itself or that pissy little paragraph at the end."
And it is a sad story, the treatment of a comedy legend by the
forgetful press and his overbearing fans, made worse by the
report of all the voices, especially since the last one hearkens
back to Uncle Ike's routine of going to Murfreesboro from his
home of Mulefoot. In the words of most comics: "That gag's
so old it's got whiskers on it." If he were trying to be funny,
he didn't succeed then and baffles now. As a distraction, the
voices worked (at the same roundtable, Szok speculated,
Myles "did" Dena Cuomo and Mandingo along with Blum
and Uncle Ike). The cousins were too stunned to follow
him. But the likely explanation, and the saddest one, is that
the master of so many voices, at this time, lost the capacity
to control them. Out of fear, for certain, but were there
occasions, under different circumstances, where the voices
simply emerged? Lamar Jackson once said, "You always got
the feeling he was listening to both what you said and how
you said it. More than once, he'd start talking to me in my
voice, then cough and shake his head. I never got mad at
him, partly because I thought he could have been joking. Or
he couldn't help himself."

Following the grocery store incident, though, people
from all over the country, having read the wire service
report, began detailing to their local and national papers

events that had happened five or ten years ago, or, in his hometown, the week before. In all, the mimic was featured as one who, without warning, slipped into the voices of others during the most ordinary hours of the day: inquiring after the cost of onions, ordering room service, asking for a light (though he never smoked). Today, one reads these accounts with incredulity, as many sound manufactured, and the makers of these allegations are those who also report extraterrestrial visits, haunted houses, and sightings of the dead: the bored, the overlooked, the emotionally needy. Many can be dismissed on the simple note that the voices alleged to have streamed out of Myles's mouths weren't in his repertoire, such as actors and politicians. (One doesn't doubt he could have done these voices had he wished, however.) Others do not correspond with his schedule, placing him in the Pelican State when his tour was leading him through the Land of Lincoln. Remaining, though, are a few, more troubling despite their small numbers; these place him correctly, attribute to him voices from routines past, but, also, and most importantly, like the "Family Hour" audience, report of obviously "different" voices that the auditors could not recognize. Perhaps it is too large a leap to suggest these people heard him uttering his family's voices, but the verdict at the time was in: Douglas Myles had crossed a line. Those old enough recalled O'Meara and his tragic last years. Fans, along with those who didn't care for mimicry, waited for the truly tragic news to emerge that revealed his complete mental removal from this world.

Whether chased there by publicity or not, now Myles's absence became complete. No longer did he simply avoid the stage, now he avoided the shopping plaza, the grocer, the post office, his sidewalk, his own porch. Those who called heard a message saying the number was now unlisted, and though he never moved or rehired security, he did stop answering his door. Fans tell of seeing a lifted blind or a parted curtain, but for the years that followed, no one who was not expected entered that house. His neighbor's children at the time of this writing report that even with this isolation, Myles did not, as most probably would, neglect his duty as a homeowner. Those who arrived to plan the restoration of his home found themselves with little repairs and maintenance, facts borne out by his personal papers, in which one can find his yearly contracts with carpenters and lawn services. One neighbor said there seemed nothing at all strange about him, in that time, save for his disappearance from life. "You'd read about it in the paper every few years, but you'd look at the house and think he was just shy or tired."

Attempts were made by the media and promoters to try and get one more interview or profile or even one more show, but after getting the phone message or receiving no invitation at his door, they found no one who could intercede on their part. The neighbors would not, nor would Lamar Jackson, who refused as a gesture to his acquaintance but as well admitted that his contacts—not due to his waning interest—had grown fewer and fewer, to the point where Xmas cards became their sole communication.

The obstacles placed before them, though, did not stop reporters—and later, the biographers and, sadly, the scholars—from speculating about the spectacular deterioration that went on inside. Paying "sources" for involved stories about the delivery of cases of liquor or posing symptoms to doctors and turning those hypotheses into diagnoses for Myles, avowing he was mute, schizophrenic, or both. It was a bad period for the reputation of Comedic Studies, especially as one of the biographers, T.K. Spaulding, was an alleged student of Chance's—he'd signed up for one of her classes, then dropped it—but most of us like to believe that today we have righted the ship.

Patricia Dunhill, who has, of contemporary Comedic Studies scholars, spent the most time studying Myles's manuscript, believes, contrary to others, that this is the time he began to write. She bases this on both physical evidence — testing of the age of the paper and ink — and by a scrupulous reading of his declarative prose. With the absence of any publishing contract — and Myles, keeper of gas station receipts, would have kept a copy — Dunhill, like others, considers the project a personal one, but she has made sense of the curious second person usage with a startling reading: that he wrote down everything that mattered in order to remember, which suggests he knew or believed he was in danger of forgetting it all. "This," she declares, "might be why there's so little devoted to the routines and the fame. Those might have been memories he didn't mind losing." To buttress her argument, Dunhill points to the manuscript itself, its well-worn edges suggesting much handling. There is, as well, in addition to the skin cell DNA, a lot of dried saliva, which may have been deposited by Myles's reading it aloud, a mnemonic tool, aided by second person address, that would keep things alive, long after he'd finished recording them. An additional insight is posited by Dunhill's mentor, Greene: that the prose, simple and unadorned as it is, mirrors his strategy for mimicry. He was reproducing, not exaggerating or parodying the events he recorded. Thus far, as of this writing, none has arrived to contest Prof. Dunhill, and, given the general competition among Comedic Studies scholars, this attests to a validity that must be afforded her argument.

Yet her research leaves an enigmatic picture, at which one might marvel or weep. The pages of the manuscript number only seventy-three, and, according to the manuscript and Jackson, Myles required but five hours at most abed. After time for eating and cleaning (the latter which he did with much fastidiousness), dressing and bathing, there still remain many hours of his day to account for. One could imagine him watching television, but for how long? Few books were found in his bedroom and in his study, and he did not go out at all, as attested to by his neighbors' children.

How then, did he spend his time? Through all the research and speculation, that one image returns, above any others, the image of Myles—better yet, the sound of him—in his house, mirroring the voices of all those he wished were near. These were the voices of the "Family Hour," a performance witnessed by these very family members when he was young, later rejected and misunderstood by those who thought at one time he was a genius. "Think how sad this is," Szok said at the roundtable. "A forlorn figure, forgotten after great fame, now the subject of ridicule. He retreats first into the world of memory, and when that fails him, he finds a method or two to keep alive those who loved him best. But the only way to attain that was to shut himself off from the real people who loved him." However, Tangier, almost immediately countered, "Why lonely? He was surrounded by the voices of the people who mattered to him most. And he was a loner by nature. I wonder if his last days differed at all from an earlier time. And I refuse to believe there's something inherently sad about the choices he may have, I emphasize, may have, made at the end. I see him, frankly, as happier than he'd been in some time, the voices, as he wrote, 'filling the emptiness with joy.'"

In her biography on Morris Gold, the late L.P. Chance claims that had the "Prince of Putdown's" widow not interceded, Gold's funeral would have been the site of an elaborate gag, where the pallbearers (unaware of their complicity) would have lifted the casket and carried it away, only to have the lid spring open, and out of it tumble a dummy who would come to a rest wearing a red clown nose and a flower that squirted water when one pressed the lapel. In his will, Gold wrote, "That'll keep them wanting more." When Douglas Myles died, at fifty-one—some, Lamar Jackson among them, say he died of melancholy—no spring-release caskets were constructed. It was believed at first that he had given us one last joke when his attorneys—who'd never met Myles—

introduced themselves as Messrs. Howe and Cheatham, but the phonebook and the Bar Association aver that those two respected gentlemen had been in practice for over thirty years. There was no funeral, despite the assertions of unauthorized biographers. No rainy burial at a gloomy cemetery, attended by few or none, depending upon the writer. As if the mimic wanted to assure, even in his death, a minimum of exposure, there would be no autopsy— to determine if he'd been born with a second larynx or a supplementary lobe in his brain. He was cremated, and with no relatives, his ashes were not collected.

Retrospectives appeared in newspapers and magazines like *The Jester*, and the ubiquitous one-hour biography appeared on television. Sales of the "History Lesson" album leapt upward and suddenly, after a long silence, one could hardly avoid hearing Myles's voice—that is, his voice doing any of his impressions. With this new popularity, the inevitable rumors of a faked death followed, its adherents using the uncollected ashes as a key to this mystery. When these quieted, Myles's popularity still grew, as those who'd heard him before and those hearing him for the first time came to appreciate how fine his talent had been, and how enduring his celebrity might be, as all sad or strange stories that accompanied his life now faded. At this time, most scholars were looking to a more distant past: Chance was working on her last book, a personal memoir of her grandfather, Lucky, Greene had finished his study over the first half of the past century, *Comics and Class: Humor's Role in Perpetuating Social Ills*, and Szok was defending his dissertation " 'The Roach Mugged the Rat for his Cheese': The Aesthetics of Social Critique," a close-reading of "Streetfighter" Archibald and Seth Finkel's *oeuvre*. Most of the essays published in journals in the years after his death are reverential, especially Greene's account of seeing the "History Lesson" and how that performance inspired the younger Greene to become a comedy historian. Gradually, though, the analysis and readings of Myles's performances started to appear, with people measuring him against his peers, those who preceded him, and the present crop of comics, those men and women who now seem to their audience as remote as the stars in the firmament, who entertain but never invite fifty patrons up on the stage. In many cases today, buying a ticket ensures one will get the clearest vision of the comic by looking at the giant video screens above, instead of the stage itself. None of the comics do mimicry now and no one has since Myles. No one wants to draw, it seems, the inevitable comparisons. Even the youngest comics today, Ansel Jenks conjectured at the recent roundtable, "don't want to be called 'the next Douglas Myles' because you can't compete with him and you fear you might end up like him."

For the scholars and those who still buy the "History Lesson," and listen as if or actually for the first time, certainly new discoveries remain. With his many mysteries—why he stopped, why he started, why he wrote the manuscript, what were his last words—it is hard to say that the search for clarity has ended, or even begun. Tangier predicts there'll never be a time in Comedic Studies when Myles won't be a prime subject of research and conversation. To wit, a young man named Deavers, a professor from Lowell Tech, has fetched some notoriety of late with a psychological analysis of the mimic as a closeted homosexual, whose inner struggle with his sexuality produced all those voices. Whether this will stand, though, remains to be seen.

In the end, can or will we ever claim to have known the man? Neither the warlock/alien/freak of the unauthorized biographies, nor the blank screen on which ideas of vogue should be projected, nor a complete mystery. Curious, forlorn, for certain; his closest companion, Lamar Jackson, near his own deathbed, said, "It's hard for me to say he knew himself." One thing is certain: Douglas Myles was a singular talent. At the roundtable, an audience member asked if there will ever be another like him, to which the scholars— Jenks, Greene, Tangier and Szok—all shouted, "No." Then, after clearing his throat, Greene said, "One wonders what Myles himself would have to say about that." Indeed, but one is left not only uncertain of what he would have said to that question, one wonders in which voice Douglas Myles would choose to speak.